WRONG PLACE,
(REALLY) WRONG TIME

IN DUE TIME

WRONG PLACE, (REALLY) WRONG TIME

by Nicholas O. Time

SIMON SPOTLIGHT

New York   London   Toronto   Sydney   New Delhi

SIMON SPOTLIGHT
An imprint of Simon & Schuster Children's Publishing Division
1230 Avenue of the Americas, New York, New York 10020
This Simon Spotlight hardcover edition September 2016
Copyright © 2016 by Simon & Schuster, Inc.
Text by Caroline Smith Hickey. Cover illustration by Stephen Gilpin.
All rights reserved, including the right of reproduction in whole or in part in any form. SIMON SPOTLIGHT and colophon are registered trademarks of Simon & Schuster, Inc. For information about special discounts for bulk purchases, please contact Simon & Schuster Special Sales at 1-866-506-1949 or business@simonandschuster.com.
Designed by Jay Colvin. The text of this book was set in Adobe Garamond Pro.
Manufactured in the United States of America 0816 FFG
10 9 8 7 6 5 4 3 2 1
ISBN 978-1-4814-7234-0 (hc)
ISBN 978-1-4814-7233-3 (pbk)
ISBN 978-1-4814-7235-7 (eBook)
Library of Congress Control Number 2016945238

CHAPTER	TITLE
1	Chance of a Lifetime

I'm hanging out in the library, minding my own business and trying to come up with something to write for my ancient history report, when our school's librarian comes up to me.

"Luis Ramirez," Ms. Tremt says, standing over me and looking down as if I'm in trouble. (I'm not, by the way. This time, at least.) "I need to speak to you about a special project. In my office."

She turns on her heel and marches to her office on the other side of the library. Immediately, I jump up from my books, fist pump, and yell, "All right!"

because, let me tell you something, the librarian at Sands Middle School is no ordinary librarian, and when she asks to see you, it isn't about something as boring as an overdue library book.

Unfortunately, I yell a little too loudly and fist pump a little too enthusiastically, because every single kid in the library turns to stare at me. I grin and shrug my shoulders at them, as if I just can't help being myself, and then dart after Ms. Tremt. When I'm inside her office, she motions with her hand for me to close the door.

"A bit more subtlety would be appreciated, Mr. Ramirez," she says, frowning. "If I'd wanted to create a scene, I could have just hollered at you from here."

"I'm sorry, Ms. Tremt," I say sincerely. "I couldn't help it. I'm so excited you chose me! I've been waiting for my turn. You have chosen me, right? That's why I'm here?"

Ms. Tremt's face cracks a smile. "I won't keep you in suspense, Luis. Yes, it is your turn."

I break into a victory dance, glad that the kids in the library can't see me. But I can't help it! Because, like I said, Valerie Tremt isn't an ordinary librarian. Valerie Tremt isn't even an ordinary *name*. It's an anagram for "time traveler," and that's what she is. Although not everyone at our school knows it, just a few of us.

I've already time traveled, by the way. Just once, with my buddies Matt and Grace. But that was really Matt's adventure, and I've been waiting patiently since then for her to choose me for an adventure of my own.

Ms. Tremt opens a locked drawer in her desk and holds up *The Book of Memories,* which is a large leather book with gold-gilded pages. Only it's not a book; it's a time-travel device. Can you believe *that*? It's not even a fancy car or a toll-booth. Just a book!

"Your classmate, Jada Reese, has just returned from her visit to 1977," Ms. Tremt explains. "So now it's your turn. I'd like you to think about what time period *you* would like to visit, and also whom you would like to bring with you, as I really don't like anyone traveling through time alone."

There's something about the way she says it that makes me curious. "How come?" I ask.

A shadow passes over Ms. Tremt's face, so quickly that it's gone before I can really be sure it was even there. "No specific reason," she replies. "Although two brains are *always* better than one. And time travel does require a person to think on their feet."

That's for sure. My first trip already taught me that when we tried to save Matt's grandfather from making a false step that would ruin his future career as a baseball player forever.

I feel a tingly sensation in my arms and legs. Is it nerves? Or are they as excited as the rest of me? "Ms. Tremt, I accept the challenge!"

She nods. "Of course you do, Luis. You're a bright young man, with a head for facts and a thirst for adventure. You leave tomorrow after school. By lunchtime tomorrow, I need you to let me know where you plan to go and with whom. I'll get the necessary wardrobe and accessories together."

I nod okay. Before I walk out, I say, "Thanks for picking me, Ms. Tremt. I know you have a lot of kids to choose from."

"You're very welcome, Luis. I do tend to lean on my best and brightest."

She gives me a wink, and feeling like I could fly if I had to, I waltz out of her office and over to my books. Tony Fracassi from my gym class looks over and whispers, "Hey, Luis, are you in trouble? Did you get yelled at?"

Grinning from ear to ear, I say, "Nope. In fact, I'm one lucky guy! And it's about *time*, too!" I laugh loudly at my private joke, and Tony rolls his eyes. I remind myself to chill out and keep Ms. Tremt's secret, or she might revoke my time-traveling permit.

I find a free computer and sit down to start researching potential time periods. There are so many amazing places I want to go. I've always wanted to see how they built the Great Wall of China, or visit the original Greek Olympics, or maybe go exploring with Lewis and Clark. How am I ever going to choose just one?

I decide to print out a bunch of pages of options and read them at home tonight. That way I can take my time and really think about it. After all, I might not get another chance. So this has to be the *best* time-travel adventure anyone has ever gone on.

As I'm printing out pages, I notice Ms. Tremt come out of her office, set up a ladder, and then begin dusting the smoke detectors with a giant purple feather duster. It's the kind of oddball thing she's known for, that and the bright, furry scarves that she wears to school every day.

"I didn't know you had to dust smoke detectors," I say as I pack up to leave.

Ms. Tremt looks at me pointedly. "Ah, well, if they go off for any reason, they set off the sprinkler system, and water is the great enemy of books, Luis, is it not? Remember that."

"Uh, sure, Ms. Tremt," I say. "I will."

"See you tomorrow, Luis. I'll be very curious to hear your decision."

As soon as school gets out, I head over to my friend Matt's house. I have to tell *someone* about my adventure and I'm hoping I can get Matt to come along. He's smart and quick and a good friend to have around when you're time traveling. (Isn't that a weird thing to think about? But it's true!)

Matt is putting a frozen pizza in the oven when I arrive. He's always starving, which is another reason I like him. "Want to shoot some hoops after I eat?"

I shake my head no, even though I'd like to.

Shooting hoops will have to wait while I make the biggest decision of my life. "Ms. Tremt told me today that I get to go next. I leave tomorrow."

Matt's face lights up. "No way! That's awesome! I wasn't sure if she was still letting kids do it. I haven't heard anything from anyone. Where are you going to go?"

I open my backpack and pull out a folder of all the pages I printed out. I have so many to choose from, but there's one that I think would not only be the adventure of a lifetime, but make the *rest* of my life more amazing too.

I slide the top sheet out of the folder and place it on the table in front of Matt.

"'The Lost Treasure of Captain William Kidd,'" Matt reads aloud. "No way. No *way!*"

See? I told you he was smart. He already gets my idea.

"I read a ton about this guy," I tell him. "He stashed stuff all over the world, and most of it was never found. This article says there's a good chance some of his treasure is still buried in New Jersey. It even names specific places, like Cape May, Toms River, and Whales Creek."

"But if people know that, and, like, there's an article *online* about it, how come it still isn't found?" Matt asks.

"Because it could be underwater, or in a man-made cave or something," I tell him. "It could be anywhere! Only Kidd knows the exact landmarks and latitudes and longitudes of the locations. People have been looking for years. They did find some stuff off the coast of Long Island a few years ago. But most of the treasure is still out there."

The oven timer *dings*, and Matt pulls out the pizza. He slices it up and hands me a piece. Gratefully, I accept it. Treasure talk makes me hungry.

"So, what's your plan exactly?" Matt asks.

This is also why I like Matt. He doesn't just tell me it's a crazy idea. He asks for my plan.

"Simple," I say. "All I need to do is go back to Captain Kidd's ship, find out exactly where he buried the treasure, and then, when I come back to the present, I'll go and claim it."

Matt snorts. "That's *all* you need to do, huh? How many times have you hung out with pirates, Luis?"

"Zero, obviously. How many times have *you*?"

"Zero," he says, taking a second slice of pizza.

"But I know this—Captain Kidd isn't going to just *tell* you where the treasure is. If it were that easy, his buddies would have all known too, and one of them would have claimed the treasure after he was dead. That was his *greatest secret*. That means he guarded it with his life."

I wipe my mouth with a paper towel and ponder this. Matt does make a good point. However, our middle school librarian is a time traveler. I, myself, am about to embark on my *second* time-travel adventure. I have seen the magical *Book of Memories* in action. Those are things that all sound impossible but that I know are true. Therefore, while it may sound impossible to find out where a pirate has hidden his treasure, I know that the impossible can be possible. If you know what I mean.

Besides, there is no *way* I'm going to let some regular old, real-life pirate stop me.

"I'll just convince him to tell me," I tell Matt confidently.

Matt shakes his head. "Luis, you're a popular guy, and everyone at Sands likes you, but this isn't a roomful of seventh graders. You're talking about sneaking onto a ship of eighteenth-century pirates, grown men who have risked their lives for this gold. And then trying to trick the smartest one of them all! It's impossible, even for you."

I shrug. I can do it; I know I can. My mom has always told me I have a big imagination, although generally she says it when I come up with some really creative story or fib to cover up something I've done wrong. And big imaginations can make big things happen.

"Matt, you are very wise," I say. "That's why I need you to come with me—to keep me from doing anything stupid."

Matt sighs. "I'd like to, man, but no thanks. I've had my adventure, and it worked out great for my grandfather and our family, but I'm done. I don't want to go again. Especially with a bunch of pirates. That's just crazy."

I decide to ignore that last comment. Matt doesn't understand how this treasure will not only change the rest of my life, but it'll make me famous, too. And I've always (secretly) wanted to be famous for something. Anything!

"Then who should I pick, if you won't come?" I ask. "Ms. Tremt said I should bring a buddy."

"A bodyguard might be more useful," he jokes. "And by the way, I'm pretty sure Ms. Tremt told us in the beginning that we can't plan a trip for selfish reasons, like winning the lottery or playing the stock market. I have a feeling treasure hunting isn't allowed either."

Oops, I forgot that. "But those things are *cheating*, you know, like using future information to go back and steal money from someone else who had rightfully won it. And this is different. No one has ever found this treasure, so it's not like taking money from someone else. It'd be helping a great national treasure be found. I can donate some to a museum if you want."

"It's not about what *I* want," Matt says. "It's what Ms. Tremt will or won't allow."

"Well, what she won't know won't hurt her, right?" I say. "After all, she's just a time traveler. Not a *mind* reader."

Matt laughs and slaps my shoulder. "That's right, Luis. She's *just* a time traveler."

"You won't come with me?" I ask again.

"Nope. But I wish you luck, buddy. You're going to need it."

CHAPTER	TITLE
2	Too Good to Be True

I head home from Matt's house, my stomach full of pizza and my head full of pirate maps and the possibility of treasure. All I need now is the right partner.

I start picturing every guy in my grade and weighing his strengths and weaknesses. There are a lot of good guys, but some are not the brightest and some are not the bravest. I need someone who is a little bit of both.

I head up to my room to start my homework, still thinking. And then it hits me like a baseball to the helmet—Patrick McMann. He just moved here recently, so I don't know him very well yet, but he's in advanced math, plays basketball, and already looks like he could be a starter on any high school football team.

I open my desk drawer to find our school's directory and look him up. He lives close to school, which is why he isn't on my bus. I pick up the phone and call him.

He answers on the second ring. "Hello?"

"Patrick?"

"Yeah?"

"This is Luis Ramirez. I'm in your math class."

There's a pause. "Um, yeah, hey."

I wonder for a second if I'm making a mistake, asking a kid I barely know to be my time-travel buddy. But then I think back to Matt's advice to bring a bodyguard, and I get this inexplicable feeling that Patrick really is the right person to bring. So I plunge ahead.

"Listen, I know this is going to sound strange, but our librarian at school is a time traveler, and she's told me I get to go on the next time-travel adventure and that I'm allowed to bring someone.

And I'd like you to come with me, since you seem like a good guy to have around when you're zipping through time."

Patrick busts out laughing. "Luis, man, you're funny. I've heard that you tell some crazy stories, but this is the craziest. Do we get to ride in a DeLorean, like that *Back to the Future* movie?"

Uh-oh. He doesn't believe me. Not that I can blame him; I didn't believe Ms. Tremt either until she showed me. I need to stay calm and sound like I know what I'm talking about.

"No, Patrick, there's no car. Ms. Tremt will tell you all about it tomorrow. We're supposed to meet with her at lunch period and tell her our destination, and then we leave after school. Will you come?"

Patrick seems to snort, or half laugh, I can't tell which. "Um, sure, okay. Why not? Isn't she that lady in the library with the really bright, fuzzy scarves? She looks kind of like Big Bird or something?"

"Yep, that's her," I say coolly. "And don't tell anyone, okay? We're supposed to keep it quiet."

"Right, sure," Patrick says. I can practically hear him rolling his eyes.

"Great! Thanks for saying yes. Get some sleep tonight. Time travel can be pretty exhausting."

"Yeah, I will. You too. Unless you're already asleep and you're sleep-calling me now? This is a dream, right?"

"Just wait," I tell him. "You'll see."

I speed through my homework, knowing I'll probably get comments from my teachers about sloppy work, but I can't help it. It's actually going to happen. I'm going to time travel again, *and* I'm going to find a lost treasure that's been missing for three hundred years!

I want to build my own regulation basketball court in the backyard with the money. My parents would agree to that, right?

At dinner, Mom notices I can hardly eat my food, even though we're having pot roast, which is one of my favorites.

"Luis, are you getting sick?" she asks, and puts her hand on my forehead. Mom always thinks I must be getting sick. If I'm tired, or not hungry, or just in a bad mood, she immediately thinks it's a vicious cold.

"No, Mom, I'm great," I tell her. "But I had a few slices of pizza at Matt's after school."

I tap my fingers on the table, and then my fork against my plate. Sitting through dinner seems so *pointless* and, well, boring, when you think about what I'll be doing tomorrow. Maybe I should do some push-ups before bed tonight, just to make sure I'm in top shape.

"Luis!" Mom says again, this time sounding really alarmed.

"What?" I blink at her. I forgot she was there for a second. I was trying to decide between whether to do twenty or thirty push-ups.

"You're fidgeting," she says. "Now I *know* something is going on. Did you get in trouble at school today?"

My older brother, Rafael, looks slyly at me from across the table. He enjoys it when I get in trouble. He's not a jerk or anything. He's actually a decent older brother. But he says he loves listening to the wild excuses I come up with to get out of things.

"I'm not in trouble! I swear. I just have a lot on my mind today, that's all."

Mom narrows her eyes. "Okay. But if I get an

e-mail from one of your teachers later, I won't be happy."

When I find five gazillion dollars' worth of treasure, you'll be happy, I tell myself, unable to stop a huge grin from spreading across my face. My brother looks at me across the table and nods knowingly, as if he's figured something out.

He couldn't know about Ms. Tremt and my plan, could he?

After dinner, Rafael comes into my room and plops down on my bed. He leans back against the wall and crosses his arms, waiting.

"Well?" he says finally, as I pretend to ignore him and pack up my book bag for school tomorrow. "You might as well tell me, Luis. Or I'll go tell Mom something's up."

"Nothing's up," I say. I try to keep my face straight, but seriously, it is so hard to lie to my brother. He knows me so well that just looking at him makes my ears turn red and the corners of my mouth pull up into a grin. Why can't I tell him? I trust him.

Rafael must see the struggle on my face

because he says, "Whatever it is, I'll keep your secret. Cross my heart and hope to die."

See how well he knows me?

With a groan, I sit down next to him and make the cross-my-heart motion. He does the same. "Here it is, Raf. You know Ms. Tremt, the new librarian?"

"Yeah, I've heard about her."

"Well, she's a time traveler."

Raf nods, smiling, waiting for a punch line, I guess.

"No, she's a *real* time traveler. Like in movies, except in real life. Her name is even an anagram for 'time traveler.'" I grab a piece of paper from my desk and show him how the letters rearrange to spell "Valerie Tremt." He smirks.

"Raf, if you're going to listen, then believe me, okay? She has a library book that's a time portal, and you can use it to travel back to anyplace in the world in any time period. I've already done it—with Matt and Grace. We went back to 1951, when his grandfather was trying out for the major leagues."

"His grandfather was a baseball player?" Raf asks. "For real?"

"Yeah, for real. Anyway, Ms. Tremt picks certain students to take turns using the portal and travel back in time. I think she wants us to experience history or something. Now it's my turn. So I've chosen to go back and meet the pirate William Kidd in the seventeenth century. I'm going to find out where he hid his treasure, because some of it is believed to be in the United States, off the coast of New Jersey, and I'm going to go and find it."

I pause to take a breath and study Rafael. He looks like he has a mouth full of toads, his cheeks puffed out and his eyes bulging. He finally spits out a laugh and rolls over onto the bed, clutching his sides and guffawing.

"Luis, you're making my stomach hurt! Man, you're the best. You really ought to be a comedian or something. You sound so serious! *I'm going to find out where he hid his treasure.* Bwahahhahahha!"

I punch his leg, hard. I can't believe he thinks I'm making this up. "I'm serious, jerk. I'm really going. And I'm going to bring something back. I'll even buy you a new phone with my treasure money."

"The latest model, right?" he jokes. "Man, Ms. Tremt a time traveler! I love it. She's kooky, that's for sure. Her outfits always crack me up."

Rafael gets up to leave my room. In the

doorway, he smiles at me. "That was a great story, Luis. You should write it down and submit it to the creative writing competition that's coming up soon at school. You'd win!"

He shuts the door, but I can still hear him cackling all the way to his room. What a jerk. I totally get why Patrick, who barely knows me, wouldn't believe me, but my own *brother*? It hurts. I never lie to Rafael. It's against the brother code.

Now I have no choice—I have to *make* him believe me. I'll bring back proof from my adventure even before I find the treasure, and I'll make Rafael eat his words.

I get in bed to read before going to sleep, and as I do, something pops into my head. In addition to the "no profiting from the past" rule, Ms. Tremt also has a rule about not *taking* anything from the past. But rules are made to be broken. Matt brought back a baseball from 1951 signed by Willie Mays! I'm sure I can figure out a way around that. I'll just take something small and pirate-y, and not valuable.

Satisfied, I pick up my copy of *Treasure Island* to help me get ready for tomorrow. There's a way around everything if you just think hard enough.

CHAPTER	TITLE
3	Patrick Is on Board

At lunch the next day, after wolfing down my food, I catch Patrick McMann's eye where he's sitting at the next lunch table. I make a small motion with my head toward the door, and he nods. Then I get up to throw my trash away and head to the agreed-upon door. He joins me in the hall a minute later, and I'm relieved, since after my talk with Rafael last night, I thought there was a chance Patrick might decide I was just looney tunes and ignore me.

"I checked the parking lot this morning but didn't see a DeLorean," Patrick jokes as we head in the direction of the library. He's talking about the car in the movie *Back to the Future* again. Ha. "Are we taking a hot-air balloon instead?"

"Ha-ha," I say. "Listen, I joke around a lot, but I'm not a liar. Just stick with me for five more minutes, and you'll see what I'm talking about, okay?"

Patrick must sense something in my voice, because he says okay and stops joking around.

I open the door to the library and walk right into George Washington and Marie Antoinette. The real ones. *For real.* In the library of Sands Middle School. I accidentally step on the hem of Marie Antoinette's gigantic ball gown, and she gives me an icy glare that makes me want to hide under a desk.

Ms. Tremt is standing behind them, looking totally frazzled and slightly sweaty. Not at all her usual self. Beside me, I hear Patrick gulp.

Ms. Tremt sees me and hurries around Marie's dress. "Hello, Luis," she says, with a glance at Patrick. I nod, indicating that he's my chosen partner.

Then, under her breath, she whispers, "They don't want to go back, Luis. Usually I can get them to return right away, but this time they're refusing. Cover for me with the other students, please!"

She turns to George Washington and Marie Antoinette. "Actors, please follow me," she says sharply. She grabs Marie by the elbow and practically hustles her out of the room. Marie looks *very* annoyed, like she might call for the *guillotine* for Ms. Tremt at any moment. Her enormous skirt swishes and bangs into furniture as she goes.

As they follow Ms. Tremt out of the library, I realize I need to do something. I turn to the students working at the computer tables who were staring and say, "Wow, cool costumes, huh? They're actors in an after-school production Ms. Tremt is directing. I was gonna try out for Washington, but Ms. Tremt said she'd already found the perfect person."

"Did you see Marie Antoinette's dress?" one girl says. "It was four feet wide! I don't know how she could walk in it."

"And her *wig* was two feet tall!" says another girl. "Our plays never have such good costumes."

"Old George had some serious body odor, though," added a boy. "He walked past me and it was like a cloud of stink. Didn't they shower back then?"

"Not as often," I say. "No indoor plumbing, you know. And, uh, Ms. Tremt likes her actors to be as realistic as possible. She's a stickler for details."

I look over at Patrick, who is stone-cold silent. I can tell by his face that he's wondering if maybe those *weren't* just actors in costumes. George Washington looked *way* too much like, well, George Washington, to be an actor. And Marie Antoinette's attitude was so . . . queenly. It's hard to think of another word for it. They were both just too perfect to be actors.

After a few minutes Ms. Tremt reappears. Her cheeks are still flushed, but she doesn't look quite so panicked. "Luis and Patrick," she says, "I have that book for you. Please, come right this way."

Ms. Tremt leads us to her office on the other side of the library. She turns to me. "I assume you have discussed everything with Patrick?"

Patrick nods. "He told me we were going to 'time travel,'" he says, using air quotes. "I don't believe him, of course. Although those actors you hired were pretty good."

"I understand perfectly," Ms. Tremt says. "You need to see proof."

Relieved I no longer have to defend my honesty, I nudge Patrick. "Just wait," I say. "You're gonna love this, I promise."

Ms. Tremt unlocks one of her desk drawers and takes out *The Book of Memories*. As soon as he sees it, Patrick reaches out and touches the cover with one finger.

"Wow," Patrick says. "That looks really old. And valuable."

"Of course it's valuable!" I say. "It's a *time-travel device*."

Patrick still looks skeptical. Ms. Tremt smiles at him and fluffs her scarf a bit. Today she's wearing a purple and neon green one, with tiny feathers sticking out of it. When she adjusts it, two feathers fall off and float down to the carpet.

She clears her throat. "Patrick, I've found that the best way to explain the book is not by *explaining it* but by giving a demonstration. Now, if you could time travel anywhere, where and when would you like to go?"

Patrick is quiet for a moment. "How about to yesterday's New York Giants game?" he asks. "They won with a touchdown in the last two minutes of the game. It was killer."

I momentarily question my choice of time-travel partner. "Patrick, seriously. We have a time machine. You can travel back *hundreds of years.* And you want to go back to yesterday?"

Ms. Tremt laughs. "It can be hard to wrap your brain around at first," she says. "But do dig a little deeper, Patrick. Luis is right—this is a custom-made demonstration just for you. Don't waste it on something you can see replayed on ESPN."

"Right, okay," Patrick says. His cheeks are red, like he's embarrassed he suggested such a thing, but he also looks frustrated, like he's sure that at any moment Ms. Tremt and I are going to laugh at him for thinking this book is really a time-travel machine, when it's actually just a dusty old book.

He chews his lip, then finally says, "Okay. We've been talking about Michelangelo a lot in history class. Can we see him painting the ceiling of the Sistine Chapel?"

"Ahh, now we're talking! He's one of my favorites." Ms. Tremt sighs dreamily and opens up *The Book of Memories.* She takes a little card out of an envelope, then signs her name, Valerie Tremt, and immediately the book sparkles and the words *Where would you like to go today?* appear on the title page.

"Whoa," Patrick whispers. "Did you see that?"

"Yep," I whisper back. "Told ya."

In careful penmanship, Ms. Tremt writes, *The Sistine Chapel, Rome, Italy, 1508.*

I suddenly remember what will happen next and tug on Patrick's sleeve to move him away from the wall with me. "Stand back," I tell him.

"Why?" he asks.

Ms. Tremt waves him back with her hand. "You'll see," she says. "Back, back."

Patrick moves back, and within seconds the book begins to shake and grow . . . and grow . . . until it's eight feet high and eight feet wide! Then, out of nowhere, an image starts to appear. It's a man lying on his back on a large scaffold, painting the ceiling of a massive church.

It's Michelangelo, and he looks to be in the beginning stages of his masterpiece.

Patrick's eyes are huge, and he shakes his head several times, as if to clear it. "Is it a photograph?" he asks. "Or a projection screen or something?"

I'm about to answer him, when Michelangelo's paintbrush starts to move. Patrick gasps.

"Keep watching," Ms. Tremt tells him. Carefully, she reaches out her hand and touches the image. Her hand disappears into the wall, *through* it, and then appears in the image, next to Michelangelo's knee.

"Wait, what—" Patrick looks stunned. He puts his hand out too, and it starts to go through the wall, touching a jar of paint. He pulls his hand back so quickly that the scaffolding shakes and the jar of paint nearly tips over. Michelangelo is startled by the noise and looks around in confusion before steadying the jar and resuming his work.

"If you wanted to, you could walk right into this scene and into the year 1508," Ms. Tremt explains. "But since this is only a demonstration, and we really *don't* want to interrupt a master, I think we should say good-bye now."

She closes the book, and we watch as it shrinks back down to its normal size. "Michelangelo is brilliant, as you know, but he can be *so touchy* when people disturb him while he's working."

Patrick is frozen with his mouth hanging open.

"So, you believe now, right?" I ask him. "You know that was real?"

"Um, yeah," Patrick admits. "I've never believed in time travel or anything. I don't even like sci-fi movies, but that . . . that was real." He looks at Ms. Tremt with an awed expression. "Could we go back there? I won't bother him. I'd just like to watch him paint for a while."

"Another time maybe," Ms. Tremt says. "Or maybe for *your* adventure. Today is about Luis's adventure. Now, tell me where you've decided to go. I saw you doing research yesterday, and I know you're a person who thinks big."

I cross my fingers behind my back for luck. I know I have to phrase this just right get Ms. Tremt to agree to it and not smell a rat.

"I've given it a lot of thought," I say. "And I'd like to go back to 1698 and sail on board a real pirate ship with Captain William Kidd."

Patrick looks at me like I'm crazy. Maybe I should have mentioned it to him in advance.

"Pirates?" he says. "*Pirates*, Luis? Why didn't you tell me that?"

"Luis, this is a highly dangerous situation you've chosen," Ms. Tremt says, studying me. She fluffs her scarf again, and more feathers drift to the floor. "I hope you realize I cannot allow you to take a trip for purely selfish reasons, such as a get-rich-quick scheme."

"I know, Ms. Tremt," I say. "That's not it at all. I just think it would be fun to be on board an actual pirate ship for a few hours. You know, swab the deck and everything. Listen to them talk. I've been reading pirate books ever since I was a little kid. I've read *Treasure Island* four times."

Ms. Tremt frowns. "Why don't I believe you, Luis?" she asks. "Time travel is perilous enough without adding bloodthirsty pirates into the mix."

"Please, Ms. Tremt," I say. I make my face look as innocent and hopeful as possible, even throwing in the big puppy-dog eyes that work on my mom. "I really thought about every place I'd want to go in history, and to be a pirate for a few hours is my ultimate dream!"

"Very well," Ms. Tremt says, her expression still more than a little suspicious. "Come back as soon as your classes are finished today and I can outfit both of you for your journey."

She pauses, taking a moment to lock the book back up in its drawer. Then she says, "And, Luis, while pirates and treasures may intrigue you, I think you'll find that you already possess a real treasure inside you. One that I hope you will discover in time."

CHAPTER	TITLE
4	Pirates Are Smelly!

The afternoon crawls by. How can I be expected to get excited about diagramming sentences or conjugating Spanish verbs when I'm about to *meet a real live pirate*? It's impossible! Or as we would say in Spanish class, *es imposible.*

I count each and every second until 3:10. When the bell finally rings, I leap up from my desk, race to my locker, and toss in my backpack and jacket. Then I walk as calmly and coolly as I can to Ms. Tremt's office, because I don't want to be seen *running* to the library. That would cause suspicion for sure, because no one has *ever* seen Luis Ramirez racing to get to the library after school.

When I arrive, I see Patrick already inside Ms. Tremt's office. They're talking, and for a second I worry that maybe he's backing out, or trying to talk her out of letting me go back to see William Kidd. At this point, I've psyched myself up so much to find out where he hid his famous treasure that I would probably cry like a big fat baby if she told me I couldn't go.

But when I walk in, they're just talking about school and she's asking him how he likes Sands and all that. *Phew.* Everything is fine. Very soon I'll be on a pirate ship in the middle of the ocean, with a bunch of dangerous and untrustworthy pirates all around me, while I try to sneakily discover the location of the greatest lost treasure in history. What could go wrong?

Ms. Tremt sees me and exhales an enormous breath. "Well," she says. "I guess this is it. Although I still don't care for the choice you've made, Luis."

I lift my chin, looking confident and mature, as I reply, "It's going to be great, Ms. Tremt, I promise."

"Very well, then," she says. "Let's go into the back room. That's where I've stashed your wardrobe." She unlocks her drawer, removes *The Book of Memories*, and places it in a tote bag, which she slings over one shoulder.

We follow her out of the office and to the very back corner of the library. There are some kids in there doing homework, but no one pays much attention to us as we follow Ms. Tremt into the back room. It has a door with no window, so no one will know that we're about to leave today and time travel hundreds of years into the past.

In the room, there's a box on the floor, and from the doorway I can smell something horrible inside of it. I put my hand over my mouth and try not to gag.

"Is that . . . *garlic?*" I ask, wrinkling my nose.

Patrick actually takes a step back and cups his hand over face. "Jeez! Is that a box of old gym socks or something? It smells worse than my brother's cleats!"

Ms. Tremt closes the door behind him and gives us a knowing smile. "I pride myself on making sure my students travel in *authentic* clothing only. The outfits here are perfect for two young boys serving as kitchen lads on a ship. And they smell because, well, you're supposed to have been on a ship for ages and there's no bathtub or washing machine available."

She reaches into the box and pulls out two sets of loose, flowy knee-length pants, striped shirts, and bright bandannas to be tied and worn on our heads. I'm hoping for a signature pirate hat, but Ms. Tremt says those wouldn't have been worn by boys in the kitchen.

Ms. Tremt leaves us alone in the room for a moment to change, and as we do, Patrick says, "So we're really doing this, huh?"

"We really are," I say. "Listen, I did this once before. It's easy. We just try to blend in, we don't say much, and we enjoy being in the past for a bit. Then we come right back. Easy peasy."

Patrick doesn't look convinced, but to his credit, he stands tall in his stinking, filthy-dirty kitchen-boy clothes and says, "Let's go, then."

I decide right then that no matter what happens on this trip, Patrick is one cool kid and I want to get to know him better.

Ms. Tremt knocks on the door, and we tell her to come in. She smiles when she sees us, but I can tell she's also holding her breath. "You boys look perfect. You'll fit right in."

"We smell perfect too, I guess," I say.

"That too." Ms. Tremt opens another box and pulls out several wacky, colorful scarves like the ones she's always wearing. She hands a couple to each of us.

"No way," says Patrick. "I'll smell like gym socks if I have to, but I'm *not* wearing that."

"Me neither," I say. "Why would a pirate wear a bright orange polka-dot scarf?"

Ms. Tremt shakes them in our faces and rolls her eyes. "Oh, boys. Haven't you figured out yet that I don't wear these scarves for fashion? They have a purpose!"

"They *do*?"

"Yes! These scarves will automatically change the clothes you're wearing to those of another time period, to help you blend in. They'll also enable you to understand and communicate in whatever language is being used. They're invaluable, really. And for this mission, I'll feel safer knowing you have them with you, even though yours are in beta phase, which means we're still testing them."

"But we can't wear them!" Patrick exclaims. "The pirates would take one look at us and think we were wackos in these nutty scarves."

Ms. Tremt ignores the implied insult and says, "That's why I had them made out of special nano-fabric, which is invisible to everyone except your fellow time travelers and compresses into a small ball. You can keep them in your pocket. Then, in an emergency, just wrap one around yourself, and you'll instantly blend in. No one will see the scarf at all. And, if you take them off, *boomf*! You zip right back to the present if you're wearing anything invented after the time period you're visiting. You can't bring anything from the future into the past. Or, at least, that's the idea."

"Then how come we can see your scarf?" I ask. I've never heard of invisible scarves that are only invisible to some people. Although I've never heard much about real time travel either, come to think of it. Ms. Tremt is like a pioneer.

"Mine are extra special," Ms. Tremt says. "The

ones I'm giving you are the new student model."

"Oh, okay, then," I say, tucking a small ball of scarf into my pocket. Patrick does the same thing.

"Are you ready?" she asks.

I look at Patrick, and he looks at me, and we both sort of shrug. I do feel authentic in my stinky pirate gear. And with the scarf in my pocket, I feel like I have a little bit of extra luck with me too.

"We're ready," I say.

"The time is now one p.m. Remember, you can only stay for three hours," Ms. Tremt warns. "If you stay longer than that, you can't travel back. Your time window closes."

"Got it," Patrick and I reply.

Ms. Tremt grins and opens *The Book of Memories*. She writes *Luis Ramirez and Patrick McMann*. Immediately the book sparkles, and the words *Where would you like to go today?* appear on the title page, just like in her demonstration. Ms. Tremt holds the pen for a moment, then writes, *February 1698, the* Quedagh Merchant.

"The *Quedagh Merchant!*" I say. "Awesome!"

I turn to Patrick to explain. "It was a rich Indian cargo ship, loaded with silks, spices, and gold. Kidd and his crew captured it, then sank their own ship, and set sail on the *Quedagh* back to the Caribbean with all of its treasure."

"So there's actual treasure on the ship?" Patrick asks. "Wow, that really *is* awesome."

"Stay clear of the treasure," Ms. Tremt warns. "If you appear too interested in it, the captain might get worried you're thieves, and trust me when I say you won't like what pirates do to thieves."

"Yes, Ms. Tremt," Patrick and I reply in unison. Ms. Tremt explains that *The Book of Memories* will start to glow when we have exactly ten minutes left in the past. We will need to find a private place to let the book grow and jump back into the present.

The book is still sparkling and shimmering, only now it's starting to grow. Ms. Tremt holds it up against the wall as it grows into a huge tableau, just as it had earlier with Michelangelo. Only this time I see a giant wooden vessel with billowing sails, and I can hear the shouts and laughter of men on board. Not just men, *pirates.*

For a second, I doubt myself. Did I just make the stupidest decision of my—

BOOMF!

I feel a jolt, and suddenly Patrick and I are standing on the deck of the *Quedagh*! There are men everywhere, manning the sails and rigging, carrying ropes, doing chores. The sea air is invigorating, and I lay my head back and close my eyes just to take it in. I can't even smell Patrick and myself anymore because we're out on the ocean, and its salty, bracing smell is completely overpowering.

In fact, I realize this is the first I've ever really *been* out on the ocean. I've been on some powerboats on rivers, or lakes, but I've never been on a real ship, let alone an old-fashioned wooden merchant ship in the middle of the ocean, with nothing around us but miles and miles and miles of water. The sight is amazing. Patrick is taking it all in too, and he looks over at me and grins, getting into the spirit of the adventure. The ship rocks and rolls with the movement of the water, and I bend my knees slightly so I can keep my balance. How do sailors and pirates sleep on ships? It must be impossible. This thing is moving constantly. It's like being on roller skates and going up and down hills, except that I'm standing still.

I move to the edge of the ship to look over the side when I feel a giant hand on my shoulder grab me and turn me around.

It's Captain William Kidd! I'm looking right up into his face, and he looks nothing like his pictures. The ones I've see online are just sketches or portraits, with him in his fancy gentleman's clothes and wig. But this is Kidd at sea, and he's in a dirty jacket and breeches, a real pirate hat on his head and a real sword by his side. A sharp one.

He doesn't look happy to see me.

"Who are ye and what are ye doing on me ship?" he growls. "Tell me quick, lad, before I throw ye overboard."

CHAPTER	TITLE
5	Moldy Bread and Treasure Maps
	3:10 p.m. (2 hours, 50 minutes left)

Kidd stares down at me, his large, hairy, pirate-y hand on my neck, and I know that it's up to me to save us. I have to think quickly and come up with one heck of a story, like Rafael always tells me I do.

Beside me, Patrick says nothing, but his face looks sick with worry. It gives me an idea.

"I'm sorry, Captain," I manage to sputter out. "Me and old, uh, Patrick, here are the new kitchen lads ye brought on in, uh, Madagascar. But we're seasick, ye see, so we've been hidin' down below, waitin' for our bellies to stop quiverin'.'"

I thank my lucky stars I reread part of *Treasure Island* last night and hope I sound like I belong on a ship. Robert Louis Stevenson better have gotten his details right, or I'm going overboard.

Kidd is silent for a moment, studying me, so I add, "We just came up on deck to get a bit of fresh air, as we're feeling a wee bit better."

Patrick jumps in. "We're ready to get to work now, Captain, if ye wish."

He sounds so perfectly in character that I want to give him a hug. Patrick McMann, Secret Pirate.

Kidd gives us both a shove in the back, not gentle, but not rough either, and snarls, "Argh! Get to work, then, laddies. And don't let me catch ye again, standing around with your hands empty, staring up at the sky. Plenty o' work on this ship, ye hear?"

"Yes, Captain!" we both shout, and I lead Patrick toward the hole in the deck where we've seen men coming up and down the ladder that leads below.

"Nice work!" Patrick whispers to me as we

scoot down the ladder into a dark hallway. "How did you come up with that story about being seasick so fast?"

"Easy—I looked at your face, and you looked like you were about to puke."

I flash him a smile as we make our way down the hallway. In the enclosed area, I can smell our clothes again, along with possibly hundreds of other bad smells. How do these pirates stand it? Do they stay up on deck on all day?

We walk right into what looks like the kitchen, which is small, with an old woodstove and shelves filled with square, wooden plates. There's a wizened old man there, dressed in an outfit very similar to ours, and he's drinking something from a dirty silver cup, and grumbling.

"Hello," I say boldly. "We're the new, uh, kitchen lads, but we've been seasick since we left port. Captain Kidd told us to report to ye and, uh, help out."

"Eh?" the man replies, cupping a hand behind his ear. He looks at us blankly.

I repeat the story, making motions that we'll

help him. He seems to be half deaf, because he finally just swats a hand at us and shrugs.

"Fine, then," he says. "Time to make supper. Ye run to the hold and bring up bags of tack, cheese, and salted beef."

"Uh, yessir," Patrick replies, standing up straight, as if he were about to salute. I do the same, and we scamper off to find the hold.

Luckily, all the books I've read about pirates taught me a few things about pirate ships. The stern, or rear of the ship, has four decks and houses the captain's quarters. The bow, the front of the ship, is the front deck, which is usually a bit higher than the rest of the top deck, to give the sailors a good view. Most of the crew have their sleeping quarters there. Some sleep in hammocks slung from the ceilings. Then below there is the kitchen, or galley, where we just were.

"The hold should be at the very bottom of the ship," I tell Patrick, as we quietly set off down below to find it.

"Will any treasure be in there?" he asks.

"Maybe, maybe not. It might be in the stores, by the captain's quarters. Although it's not like we can carry around trunks of gems or silks without being caught."

Patrick looks at me oddly. "I wasn't asking because I think we should *take* some," he says. "I was asking so that we can *avoid* it."

"Right, of course," I say. What am I thinking? I was actually just considering running to the ship's stores to steal a bar of gold or an ingot! I must be crazy. Treasure crazy.

Down in the hold, we find the bags of food and haul them back up to the galley. The cook shows us what to do, and we start setting out the strange, square plates for the pirates to come through and grab their supper. They'll take the food up on deck to eat at one of the long tables set up there. Even after reading about pirate food, seeing it and touching it in person is worse.

Patrick can't believe how hard the cheese is. "It's like rocks," he says, handing chunks of it to the men as they go by. "And the creepy crawlies coming out of the biscuits! They don't seriously eat them, do they?"

I nod. "They do. They're weevils—it's protein. Otherwise the salted beef is pretty much all they have for protein, unless they have livestock on board."

When everyone is served, the cook motions for us to go up on deck and eat with the men. I can't wait to go, since the smell in the kitchen is even worse with the food around. Patrick and I each take a wooden plate up and sit down on the deck, since there isn't room at the long tables.

"This is where the expression 'three square meals a day' comes from," I tell Patrick. "They use square plates because carpenters make them on the ship, and the square shape is quick and easy to make. And they use wood because they won't break if they get tossed around, like china."

"How do you know so much about all of this stuff?" Patrick asks, nibbling carefully at a piece of the cheese. "No wonder you wanted to come here. I thought you really wanted treasure, like Ms. Tremt said, but now I think you're pirate obsessed."

"I am, I guess," I say, laughing.

Patrick picks up his hardtack to eat next, and a pirate comes rushing over. "No, lad! Like this."

He picks up the biscuit and thumps it hard against the deck's floor. "Ye can tell how old it is by tappin' it. If the bugs crawl out quick, and look fat and white, then there's still some nutrition left in the bread. But if they come out slow and look old, then they've eaten all that's good in it, and ye might as well turn it into a belt buckle."

I look over at some of the men at the table. While some are eating, some are, in fact, carving their biscuits into belt buckles and their cheese into buttons.

I bang my hardtack onto the deck and a bunch of young, healthy weevils crawl out. The pirate smiles at me, half of his teeth missing, the other half worn down from eating such hard food, and he motions that I should go ahead and eat it.

Patrick looks horrified, but I force myself to put it to my lips and take the smallest, mouse-size bite. The men cheer and bang their cups on the table. "Welcome to the sea, laddies!" they shout.

Patrick does the same and he's met with more cheers. He shoots a side glance at me, and we smile. Maybe the world has misjudged pirates. They're not bloodthirsty scalawags! They're decent men who have been roughed up by the hard life at sea, sleeping in a rocking hammock, never bathing, and eating this terrible, old, hard food. No wonder they aren't as easygoing as everyone else. But they're good guys underneath.

I breathe a sigh of relief that I didn't pick us a death-wish adventure after all.

When the men are done eating, Patrick and I clean up the plates and scraps and return them to the kitchen. The old cook waves us off, and we leave the galley.

"That was fun," Patrick says. "I thought this was going to be terrifying, but actually, these are nice guys. And being on a ship is neat! I want to write a paper about it for history class, but I guess that would be kind of odd, right?"

"I think so. I mean, how would you explain *really* knowing what it was like to be on a seventeenth-century pirate ship?"

"Good point." Patrick scratches his head. "How much time do we have left? Maybe we should go back."

"Sure." Then, because I just can't help myself, I say, "Let's take one last look around before we go. After all, we'll never get another chance to be on a ship like this."

Patrick nods. I can see he's curious what else we'll find too. "Okay, just for a minute. I guess it wouldn't hurt just to *look*."

"Right, exactly."

What I don't tell him is that what I *really* want to do is try to sneak down to the hold or the captain's quarters and see if I can find a piece of treasure. I had been making excuses the entire time we were in the kitchen, but I kept being called back every time I tried to sneak away. I want to find something *really* small, like a single doubloon, that I can tuck in my pocket and bring back to the present as proof to show my brother. And if I happen to see a map of where Kidd plans to hide the treasure from this ship, then so be it. . . .

I lead us slowly toward the stern of the ship, where I know Kidd's room will be. As we near the door, I pause, listening. There's no sound coming from inside or anywhere near it, so I take a chance and lead Patrick into the room. It's empty! And it's without a doubt the coolest place on the ship.

Since the *Quedagh* is a merchant vessel,

which is massive and designed to hold a lot of cargo, Kidd's quarters are impressive. They are nicely furnished, with a bed, a desk, and a table and chairs for about six people. There's a stack of books and other interesting things lying about. But it's his desk I want to investigate.

I inch toward it, and Patrick grabs my arm. "We've got to get out of here, Luis. I'm sure Kidd'll be back soon, and if he catches us . . ."

I shake his hand off. I'm not going to miss my chance. This is why I came on this adventure to begin with! Not to serve drinks and weevily bread. "He's probably up on deck with the men," I tell him. "This'll just take a second. I want to see where this ship is heading."

On top of the desk is a detailed map of the Indian Ocean, with arrows and ships and routes drawn all over it. I can't figure out what it all means exactly, except that it seems to be a record of which ships they spotted while in the Indian Ocean, possibly where they overtook the *Quedagh*.

I open up a few drawers, hoping to find something else, but only find more maps of the tip of Africa, routes to England, et cetera. No maps of the United States, which is where historians are nearly certain he put most of the *Quedagh's* treasure. Although it's possible that Kidd originally planned to put it somewhere else and changed his mind later, when he got back to the British colonies in North America and found out he was wanted for piracy. He doesn't know that yet, and won't for a few more weeks.

Patrick is standing nervously against the wall, keeping a lookout. The ship pitches back and forth as the ocean gets a bit rougher, and he accidentally slams his shoulder into a picture hanging on the wall by the door. The picture falls to the floor with a *bang!*, revealing a small hidden door behind it.

"Holy hardtack, Patrick! You did it!" I yell, running over. I reach up to open the little door, positive it contains all of Kidd's secrets. Why else would a pirate have a hidden cubby in his office?

Inside, I see a single rolled-up scroll. It's the treasure map! I know it. I can feel it in my bones. I reach inside and pull out the scroll, realizing as I do that it's got a thin, nearly invisible string tied around it, and as soon as I pull it out, there's a strange noise, like a *whiiiiiiiiisssst!*

"Get back!" I shout to Patrick, and we both leap away from the wall. At that exact second, a butcher knife falls from the ceiling and buries itself in the floor. If we hadn't moved, I would have lost my hand!

"It's a pirate booby trap!" I exclaim, delighted. I've always wanted to see one, and now I have. I'm not even scared, because I'm so excited to have the map in my hand and my hand still attached to my body. "This is awesome."

"Umm, maybe we should go? Like, right now?" Patrick suggests tersely, his face red.

"Yes," I say. "Good idea. Get the b—"

But my words are cut off as Captain Kidd storms into the room, takes one look at me holding his map, and grabs us both roughly by the neck.

"THIEVES!" he shouts, and all at once, the pirates on the ship start yelling.

CHAPTER	TITLE
6	More Time Travel Than We Bargained For
	4:40 p.m. (1 hour 20 minutes left)

Kidd and another pirate, who came running as soon as Kidd started shouting, drag us up to the deck, where Kidd begins to question us in front of the crew as if we were on trial or something.

"Are ye English spies, then?" Kidd asks, leaning in close to my face.

His breath and his body both smell terrible, despite him being slightly cleaner and in nicer clothes than the other pirates. The fumes are clouding my brain and I can't think. He wrenched the map out of my hands as soon as he caught us, so I didn't have a chance to glance at it. If only I'd gotten one quick look! I could have at least found a landmark or a town name. Now my chances of finding treasure are ruined.

"Tell me who ye are!" he growls.

"We're not spies!" Patrick declares, and I'm amazed at how cool he sounds. "We're, you know, kitchen lads."

I start shaking. I can't help it. Things have gone very, very wrong. But this is my adventure, and I brought Patrick here, so it's up to me to save us. I just need to think of a plan.

Plan B, Plan B, where are you? I wonder. My brain doesn't usually take this long. I blame the fear racing through my mind and body odor.

Kidd looks at his crew for a ruling, as if they are the jury. "What say ye, men? Are they kitchen lads? Or spies? Will anyone vouch for these boys?"

The pirates, who only half an hour earlier had been hanging out with us and joking around up on deck, immediately turn against us. They shake their heads no and look at us with disgust.

"They're spies! Both of 'em!" one calls.

The guy in charge of the kitchen points at me and says, "He was trying to shirk his kitchen duties and run off. Up to no good, I'm sure!"

Another, the pirate who showed Patrick how to bang his hardtack, says, "They were snoopin' about! They were nosin' everywhere!"

A third one, with a big red nose and an eye patch, shouts, "Make 'em walk the plank, Cap'n!"

Out of the side of his mouth, Patrick mumbles, "These pirates are jerks! They loved us at supper. Got any bright ideas, Luis? C'mon! You're Mr. Creative. If there was ever a time for one of your brilliant excuses, it's *now*!"

I close my eyes for a second. I'm a strong swimmer, but no one can stay afloat in the middle of the Indian Ocean for long. There are no ships on the horizon, and who knows if it'd even be safe to climb aboard one? We have to stay on this ship, and we have to go somewhere alone so we can use the book. And fast.

"Don't worry. I'll think of something," I say, trying to sound confident. Should I ask to use the bathroom? *Um, excuse me, Captain Kidd, but I really, really need to pee.*

Kidd looks deep into my eyes for a second, as if he's searching for something. Then he stares into Patrick's. He wouldn't really make two *boys* walk the plank, would he? That would make him a pretty ruthless captain. Although, considering he amassed one of the largest unfound treasures in the world, it's likely that he *was* a pretty ruthless captain.

"Laddies, ye were caught red-handed with me map. No one will vouch for ye. Ye'll have to walk the plank." He gives Patrick a shove with one meaty hand. "Ye first."

Patrick looks like he might faint. He inches over to the plank, which two helpful pirates are quickly shoving out off the edge of the deck.

"*Help,*" Patrick squeaks as he moves closer to it. Ordinarily, I'd yell "Run!", but that's the problem with pirate ships. There's nowhere *to* run.

I have no time for a fancy, creative plan. I have to act *now.* I know I'm not allowed to show anyone *The Book of Memories* while we're time traveling, but I'm pretty sure that in life-and-death situations, rules can be broken. In any case, I can argue about it with Ms. Tremt later.

Right now I need to save Patrick.

I whip out the book from my back pocket and scrawl our names, *Sands Middle School*, and today's date in the present.

"Patrick, catch!" I yell. Then I quickly toss him the book.

He catches it neatly. I don't even let myself think about what could have happened if it had fallen in the ocean!

"What's this?" Captain Kidd asks, narrowing his eyes. "More things from me office?"

"No, no, this is my, um, diary," Patrick says. "Do you mind if I read a passage from it before I, uh, plunge to my death?"

Kidd looks annoyed, but he acquiesces. "I suppose I'll grant your last request. But make it quick."

Patrick glances at me, and I nod quickly, indicating that I'll be ready.

Patrick opens the book on the plank, and I watch in delight as the jaws of Kidd and his crew drop as the book begins to shake and grow. Once it's large enough for Patrick to enter, he shouts, "See ya, pirates! Back to the present, here I come!"

He disappears into the book, and without even allowing myself one last look at the *Quedagh Merchant*, I leap up onto the plank and dive into the book after him. I'll miss 1698, but it's not worth drowning in the—!

BOOMF!

We land hard. I shake my head a bit to clear it and see Patrick beside me, doing the same thing. When I look up, I realize that something's wrong. Wherever we are, it doesn't look at *all* like the library of Sands. In fact, it looks a lot like where we just were!

We're on a ship. On the ocean. Still. Only it's not the *Quedagh Merchant*, it's at least thirty degrees colder, and the men on the deck don't look like pirates. In fact, they look like . . .

"*Vikings?*" Patrick asks, his voice rising up an entire octave.

I study them. They have to be. The men are tall, mostly blond and red-haired, and have neat, trimmed beards. And they're wearing helmets with horns on top, and some of them have swords.

We've landed on a Viking ship.

"Is this how it's supposed to work?" Patrick asks.

"No!" I reply as the Vikings begin to take notice of us standing on their deck in pirate kitchen-lad gear.

"So, then, do something!" he says. "You're the one who's supposed to be the time-travel expert!"

"I never said I was an expert!" I snap. "Just, um, put your scarf on. Let's see if they work."

He does, and I do the same. Whether or not they actually make us blend in with the others on the ship, I don't know. But it gives me some comfort to wear it, even though mine is bright pink and as furry as a sheepdog.

"Now let's take them off at the same time," I instruct. "Ms. Tremt said they'd automatically send us home if we did that because we are wearing clothes from the wrong time period."

We yank off our scarves on the count of three, but nothing happens. I do hear some sort of sputtery noise, but we stay put.

I stare at Patrick. "We're supposed to get bounced right back to the library if we take these scarves off! What's going on?"

Patrick blinks at me. "Um, apparently these don't work *quite* the way she thought they did. . . ."

And if the Vikings could see our pirate clothes we should bounce back home. But still, nothing happens. I gulp hard.

"Arggh! Let's try the book again, then!" I flip my scarf back around my neck, since I don't have time to ball it up properly, and open the book. Suddenly I catch sight of a thin, dark-haired man in a long leather coat who looks completely out of place.

"Who's that guy?" Patrick asks. "He doesn't belong on a Viking ship."

"Neither do we!" I say, scribbling our names and the school's name and the date in the book once again. This time I underline *Sands Middle School.* Just as the book is growing big enough for us to leave, I glance up at the man and see that he's coming toward us, waving a big green, gloved hand at us. "Wait!" he calls, tripping over the foot of a very large Viking. The Viking howls.

But we can't wait; it's not safe. So we jump into the book and . . .

BOOMF!

I can't believe it. It's wrong *again*! The smell of sea air is gone, and for a moment I'm just thankful we're not on another ship. Ships have planks. Ships have nowhere to run. Instead, we're in the . . . desert?

"The desert?" Patrick announces. "Seriously? What did you write, Luis?"

"I wrote 'Sands' and underlined it!"

"Well, smooth move," he says sarcastically. "There's plenty of *sand* here. Now can you get us to Sands *Middle School*, please? I think I'm done with time travel. For now. For*ever*."

I shake my head. "You don't understand—I wrote *Sands Middle School*. I wrote that the first time too. And it's how I got back before, with Matt and Grace. Something's wrong. Something isn't working right."

"Isn't that a pyramid?" Patrick asks, shading his eyes and pointing ahead of us.

I squint and try to see. Believe it or not, because everything in the desert is sand-colored and the sun is so strong, it's actually hard to see a pyramid even when it's not that far away from you. In front of the pyramid is a parade of people carrying a boy in a chair above their shoulders. The boy has on a huge gold headpiece. Could it be someone royal?

"At least no one here is going to hurt us," I say. "So we've got that going for us."

"True," says Patrick. "But what if the book is broken? The scarves can't get us back. Will we be stuck here forever if we miss the three-hour deadline?"

"Um, I hope not. I don't think so. I hope not." I can barely get the words out. That had never seemed like a possibility to me before. Stuck in Ancient Egypt? Would it be so bad?

Yes, I decide, it would. I already feel the hot sun burning me, and I'm awfully thirsty. I look around and see absolutely no roads to anywhere. Definitely no nearby convenience stores with soda and sunscreen.

"Hey, who *is* that guy?" Patrick asks, pointing. "He was on the Viking ship!"

I squint again and see the man in the leather jacket and green gloves. I can't believe it. He looks just as out of place in the desert as he did on the Viking ship. If he's here *and* he was on the ship with us, does that mean he's time traveling too?

"Oh my gosh! He's a time traveler!" Patrick says at the exact moment I think it. "Right? Isn't that right? How else could he be here too?"

"I have no idea. Are there a bunch of other time travelers out there?"

Patrick shrugs. "Who knows? But I don't like the look of that guy. He isn't a nice librarian lady like Ms. Tremt. Let's try to get out of here before our time limit runs out."

The man spots us and immediately begins hurrying toward us, just as he did on the ship. He's yelling something, only the desert is windy and I can't hear what he's saying. But somehow I know the man is bad news and we don't want him anywhere near us.

I open the book and very carefully write our destination for the third time. It *has* to work this time. It has to.

BOOMF!

I'm almost afraid to open my eyes. When I finally do, it's only because I hear Patrick let out a loud groan beside me.

"Wrong again," he says. "We're *onstage*, Luis!"

I open my eyes, and I'm nearly blinded by the lights. We *are* on a stage, and there are actors beside us, pantomiming some kind of brawl.

Luckily, they're too busy to notice us. We still have our Tremt scarves on, which hopefully means we look like actors too, although now I'm doubtful they work at all. Patrick grabs my arm and pulls me off the stage.

I'm stumped. Why can't we seem to get home? Why do we keep landing in weird times and places when I'm writing our destination so carefully?

And why didn't Ms. Tremt warn me this could happen to us? Maybe I would have rethought this whole adventure.

"*What* is going on?" I moan.

"Don't freak, Luis, but I think I see that leather-jacket guy again," Patrick says, peeking out through the curtain.

A minute later there's a ruckus on the other side of the stage curtain and I hear a voice.

"But I *must* get back there," the voice whines. "My two sons are there, and I have to see them."

"I'm sorry, sir," a voice with an English accent replies. "No audience members backstage."

"I think that's him!" I whisper. "And he's trying to find us! Why?"

"Maybe he wants to help us," Patrick guesses. "Although I doubt it. There's something so strange about us not being able to get home and him appearing everyplace we land. Let's try the book one more time. And let's put our scarves back on—hopefully they will work this time and we won't look like smelly pirates when we land back at school."

"Okay, but we have to do something different this time," I say. "It's our fourth try." I begin writing our destination, but this time I add an *SOS* next to it as a cry for help. Hopefully Ms. Tremt can read it, or sense it, or her scarf will start beeping or something.

"Concentrate *really* hard on school, okay?" I tell Patrick. "Picture school. *Will* yourself to land at school."

"Believe me, I am."

"Ready?" I hold up my hand, fingers crossed. Patrick does the same. The book starts to shake and grow, and we step into it together. I close my eyes and visualize the Sands Middle School library and hope that's what I'll see when I open them.

CHAPTER	TITLE
7	The Book Thief
	5:57 p.m. (three minutes left)

BOOMF!

Petrified, I open my eyes, and almost collapse in a heap of joy when I see shelf after shelf of books. We made it! There are even a few kids still sitting at computers, which means even though it felt like we were gone for hours, it must have been only minutes. Ms. Tremt hurries over to us, fluttering and flapping like a bird.

"Boys, boys, this way. I have those microfiche sheets for you. Right in here." She nods sharply, and we follow her to the back room. Patrick shoots me a look of utter relief that we're home. If Ms. Tremt weren't in such a hurry to get us to the back room and away from everyone's eyes, we'd probably hug.

Once the door is shut, Patrick asks, "What's microfiche?"

Ms. Tremt shakes her head. "Never mind that now. Smart of you to put your scarves on for your return! You look like you're in regular school clothes. I'm not sure how much longer I can tell people I'm putting on a play that never seems to happen!"

She makes a clucking sound and puts her arm around me in a half squeeze, and I realize that she was actually scared for us.

"Ms. Tremt, what happened?" I ask. "How come we got stuck?"

"That's what I want to ask *you*! I got your SOS, Luis, and pulled you back immediately. But what was the danger?"

Patrick looks at me, but I motion for him to go ahead and explain. Now that we're back, I'm feeling even more shaken than when we were gone.

"We kept trying to come back and landing in different times," Patrick explains. "A Viking ship, Ancient Egypt, and then a vaudeville stage. We couldn't get here. We even tried taking off the scarves, but that didn't send us home either."

Ms. Tremt snaps her fingers. "Darn it! I knew they still needed testing. At least they make you blend in though."

"But that's not the weirdest part," I interject. "There was a man who followed us to each place!"

Ms. Tremt sucks in a breath, and a bright red flush creeps up her cheeks. She puts a hand to her throat. "A man?" she asks. "What did he look like?"

"He had on a long leather coat," I say.

"And had dark, oily hair," Patrick adds.

"And bright green gloves," I say, thinking this was the most important detail of all. "And he was always running toward us, telling us to wait. Or tripping over something. But he wanted to talk to us."

"Ah," Ms. Tremt says. "Thank you for letting me know." She blinks nervously for a minute. "I'm going to go do some research in my office now. How about you boys change and head home to start your homework? It's about the same time as you left, so your parents will be expecting you home from school any minute."

"Yes, Ms. Tremt," we both reply.

At the door, she pauses. "Luis, I assume you learned a thing or two about pirates on your trip."

"I did, Ms. Tremt," I say. "And I never want to see one again."

"Me neither," Patrick says, shuddering. "But thank you both for including me in this trip. I never want to do it again, but it was the adventure of a lifetime, that's for sure."

"I'm glad you're both safe." Ms. Tremt smiles at us and shuts the door, leaving us to change.

Patrick and I put on our regular, not-disgusting, smelly clothes, and begin reliving some of the highlights of our trip. In the safety of the library, it's already becoming a memory. As we grab our backpacks to leave, I see *The Book of Memories* still sitting on the table. Our nano-scarves are there too, rolled up into their tiny balls. Ms. Tremt must have been so flustered by our mention of the strange man, or the SOS we sent, that she forgot to collect them from us.

Patrick walks out of the room ahead of me, apparently unaware of the tremendous gift Ms. Tremt has left me. She warned me on my first trip with Matt that the book should never be taken out of the library. I assume the same is true of the scarves. But these are extenuating circumstances.

Maybe I didn't find a treasure map today, and I won't be the person to discover Captain Kidd's long-lost treasure, but I will have something to show for our trip. Proof for Rafael that I'm not just a storyteller—I've really been to the past.

I hastily scoop up the scarves and the book and slide them into my backpack. I'll return them to Ms. Tremt tomorrow, after I've proved my brother wrong.

As I'm walking home from school, I can't help feeling like maybe my pirate adventure isn't quite over yet.

At home I start my schoolwork and wait for Rafael. I'm distracted, and all I can think about is how close I was to finding out where Captain Kidd was planning to put the *Quedagh Merchant* treasure before I let it slip out of my hands. Literally.

My dad calls me down to dinner around six, and I expect to see Raf at the table. Instead, it's just me and my parents.

"Where's Raf?" I ask, disappointed.

My dad eyes me suspiciously. Raf is always off somewhere—at a friend's house, at basketball, et cetera. It's not like me to be disappointed or surprised not to see him.

"He's over at Jack's house and won't be home until late," he says. "Why?"

I shrug, oh so casually. "Just curious. I have a homework question."

"I can help, if you want," Dad offers. He takes a large enchilada from the casserole dish Mom has just pulled from the oven. They smell delicious and remind me of just how awful that pirate food really was. Those bloodthirsty pirates might have behaved completely differently if they'd been allowed to eat my mom's cooking!

"Dinner smells awesome, Mom," I say. For the first time in my life, I realize how lucky I am to have parents who cook me a hot, tasty meal every night. "Those enchiladas look so good, I could eat five. Or ten. I might even write a poem about them."

Mom laughs. "Flattery will get you everywhere. And you *should* write a poem, Luis. You've always had a way with words. Even when you were little. Once, when you'd flushed a lipstick of mine down the toilet, I asked you why you did it, and you told me the lipstick color just wasn't pretty enough for your mama, so you tossed it."

I start laughing, and my dad joins in. I don't remember that at all. I feel a little bad about it, actually. "Sorry, Mom."

She waves her hand. "Oh, it's all right. You were so adorable when you said it that I forgave you immediately. That's always how it's been with you, Luis. You're so creative and funny, it's impossible to stay mad at you."

Dad grins. "Well, not *impossible*. I was pretty mad the day you borrowed my bike without asking and blew out both tires."

All three of us erupt into laughter. "I'm a very responsible kid," I joke.

"That reminds me," Mom says. "Dad and I both have early meetings tomorrow morning, so you and Raf will have to get yourselves fed and dressed and off to school without us. Okay? And no shenanigans—even funny ones. Got it?"

"Got it," I say. But inside I feel a flutter of excitement. With my parents both out of the way in the morning, it'll be the perfect time to show Raf *The Book of Memories.* Maybe I can even give him a quick demonstration. I won't go anywhere, not with that wacky green-gloves man out there, but I could show something from history, like Ms. Tremt did with Patrick and Michelangelo. That would be harmless enough.

I finish my homework after dinner and place the book on my desk, so that I'll be ready to show it to Raf first thing tomorrow. I fall asleep quickly in my warm bed, glad I'm not a hungry pirate swinging in a hammock on the *Quedagh Merchant.*

CHAPTER	TITLE
8	Uninvited Guests

I wake up to the sound of something rustling in my room. It sounds like a mouse. Or maybe several mice. Groggy, I peer into the darkness, where I see a person hovering over my desk. It's so dark I can't tell who it is, but the noises continue. It's got to be my brother trying to steal some candy from the secret stash in my drawer. He always waits until I'm asleep to sneak in.

"Rafael!" I growl. "Get out of my room! I'm sleeping!"

The person doesn't answer. Instead I hear a

voice muttering something like, *Finally! Finally! I'll have the power to bring everyone here!*

Is that voice in my head or in my room? Am I awake or dreaming?

"Raf!" I say again. "Get out or I'll tell Dad!"

My dad must hear me yelling, because a second later he's at my door, knocking. "Luis? Is everything okay?"

And just like that, the noises stop and Rafael disappears. He must have crawled out of the room or something.

"I'm fine, Dad," I mutter. "G'night." Still half-asleep, I roll over and pull my pillow down over my ears. I fall back to sleep immediately.

I'm on the pirate ship again. This time, I'm walking the plank, not Patrick. It's even scarier than it looked when I was watching him. The plank is wobbly, the ocean is rough, and the pirates are hoping I'll fall at any second. I look around for the book to save myself, but the book isn't in my pocket. I look over at Patrick, standing on the deck beside Kidd, but he doesn't have it either.

"Where's the book?" I shout, but no one answers.

Then Kidd waves his hand to indicate I should jump off, and I see that he's wearing a pair of bright green gloves. . . .

Green gloves.

"Fhfdusirhw!" someone shouts in my ear.

I sit up in bed with a start. What was that? I was dreaming I was back on the *Quedagh*, just about to drown, and then . . .

Someone leans in close to my face and shouts at me again. "Fhfdusirhw!" he yells. The boy is wearing an elaborate gold headpiece. He's shirtless, his only clothing a heavy gold skirt thing.

I blink a few times to make sure I'm not still dreaming. But I'm in my room, and I'm in my bed. And yet somehow there's an *Egyptian* pharaoh standing beside me, shouting at me. And I'm pretty sure some of his spit just landed on my cheek.

Yep. This is real.

I study his angry, red face. He's young and dressed like a king. He's got to be King Tut. *King*

Tut. In my bedroom! How is this happening?

Tut yells at me again, which isn't very helpful, since to my ear it sounds like gibberish. I grab the balled-up hot pink nano-scarf off my bedside table and wrap it around me so I can understand him. Hopefully its translation powers work better than its send-people-back-to-the-present powers.

"I'm hungry!" King Tut says, clear as day. Yay for Ms. Tremt! At least the scarves do something. "Make me food, *now*."

"Uh, what do you want?" I ask, stalling for time. What do I do? I remember Ms. Tremt had a problem the other day with George Washington and Marie Antoinette coming into our time and then refusing to leave. But that was at school. Where the time traveling happens. Not here at my *house*.

I hear a loud *thud* from my closet and look over. There's a large, burly man combing through my clothes and tossing items out onto the floor. He's just grabbed my baseball bat and clunked it against the wall. He's wearing fur and a large horned helmet. He has a neatly trimmed beard.

Oh no, I think. *No, no, no, no, no, no.*

"YAAAARGH!" the Viking roars. He tosses my clothes on my bed. "These are too small! I need bigger clothes. Get me some."

My head starts spinning. King Tut and a Viking are in my bedroom, which now has a slight stench. I'm pretty sure the Viking is responsible for it.

A second later another man appears in my doorway. He's much smaller than the Viking, and he's wearing my dad's tracksuit. He also has on a black bowler hat and has a small black mustache, and looks oddly familiar.

"These clothes fit *me* quite nicely," he says with a smile and an English accent. "However, they're a bit casual for my taste. And where in the world do you keep your hat boxes?"

I gasp. It's all becoming clear now. Vaudeville, the Viking ship, the Pyramids. A person from each place we visited yesterday has come *here*!

The man with the mustache does a little pantomime routine, pretending he's tripping and falling over, using his hat as a prop.

"Are you Charlie Chaplin?" I ask him. My mom loves Charlie Chaplin movies. She'll sit in the TV room with a huge bowl of popcorn and watch these old, *silent,* black-and-white movies and laugh her face off. It's bizarre.

The man bows. "Indeed I am. A pleasure to make your acquaintance."

"Boy!" yells King Tut again. "Make me some food now, or I'll have you sacrificed to the gods. And you won't like it."

"Yaaargh! Where is your gold?" yells the Viking. "Show me now!"

Suddenly, I spy *The Book of Memories* on my desk. Only it's lying open, when I'm positive I left it closed last night.

Then it all comes back to me, and I remember the noises over my desk in the middle of the night. Rafael must have snuck in for candy, opened the book, and then . . .

But wait. No. That isn't it at all! It was the green-gloves man! Someone was muttering something odd in my room, and then when my dad came the person disappeared. And then I had the dream about the green gloves on Captain Kidd.

I start to freak out a bit. It was scary enough yesterday when he was following us from time to time, but to have him in my *room*? He must want the book, and he thought he could steal it easier here. I need to get it back to the library and to Ms. Tremt as soon as possible.

The Viking picks up my belt and bites into it, leaving teeth marks. "Good leather," he mutters. "Did you make it?"

I slap my hand against my head. Somehow I've really made a mess of my time-travel adventure. Was it the green-gloves man who ruined everything? Or was it because I was greedy and trying to steal Kidd's treasure that set off a chain of bad events? Ms. Tremt did say there were rules to time travel.

I don't have the answers, but I *do* know that I need to deal with these uninvited guests ASAP.

Charlie digs out my baseball hat collection and starts trying several of them on. King Tut grabs one and chews on it, then spits it out. The Viking tosses one up onto the tip of his sword and then performs a trick, sort of like spinning a basketball on one finger, where he spins the hat on the tip. Then Charlie spies my laptop on my desk and hurries to pick it up.

"Put that down!" I plead, but he's shaking it like a baby rattle and holding his ear to it, trying to figure out what it is.

I throw my hands up in the air and decide I can't handle this myself. It's time for reinforcements.

Thankfully, my parents are already at work. I remember mom saying they both had to go in to work early today. At least I can deal with this without getting in trouble. I hope.

I walk down the hall to Raf's room and burst in without knocking. He's fast asleep in his bed, despite all the yelling and banging coming from my room.

I walk over and give his shoulder a shake. "Get up, Raf! I need you."

He mutters something in his sleep and swats me away without even opening his eyes.

I try again, this time giving him a really hard shove. "Raf! Help!"

He sighs and rolls onto his back, groaning. "It's early, Luis. Can't I have ten more minutes?"

"No, because we have an emergency. Look."

I point toward his doorway, where the Viking

has appeared, having followed me from my room. He's carrying my lucky baseball, which he throws with surprising speed at my head. I duck. It bounces off the wall over Raf's dresser, nearly breaking the mirror before finally landing on the floor.

"Bad Viking," I say, shaking a finger at him. "Don't throws things in my house, okay?"

He looks remorseful for a second, but then picks up Raf's trash can and begins digging through it.

King Tut elbows his way around the Viking and marches up to me. "I'm still hungry, boy, and I'm about to have you dismembered for dis-obedience."

Rafael gasps.

"There are some people I'd like you to meet, Raf. This is King Tut, and that's a Viking, although I don't know what his name is, and the dude with the hat and cane in the hallway there is Charlie Chaplin. Now get up, and help me get rid of them!"

CHAPTER	TITLE
9	King Tut Wants a Snack

Where did you *find* these people?" Rafael asks. "And why did you bring them here?"

I shake my head. "I *didn't* bring them here, obviously. Look at them! Ms. Tremt is a time traveler. Yesterday she let me and Patrick McMann use her magic time-travel portal, and we visited one of Captain Kidd's pirate ships. We were almost killed when he made us walk the plank, but we escaped with our lives."

Rafael sighs. "Not that again."

"*Yes*," I insist. "That again. But then there

was *another* time traveler chasing us on the way home, and he made us land in a bunch of different times, like Ancient Egypt. And I sort of snuck home Ms. Tremt's *Book of Memories* and left it on my desk last night so I could show you and *prove* that everything I've been saying is true, and *then*, I think the time-traveler guy snuck into my room and opened the book last night and let these guys in."

Rafael sits up and scratches his head. The Viking has one of Rafael's large Lego models in his hand and he's dangling it from his fingers like bait on a fishhook.

"Be gentle with that!" Rafael yells. The Viking ignores him.

I hand Rafael the other nano scarf I still had from yesterday. "Put this on. It's a nano-scarf. It'll help them understand you, and you'll be able to understand them."

"A nano what? I've got to be dreaming," Rafael says. "Or, you are the worst little brother."

"You're not dreaming," I reply. "Listen, I've got to make some breakfast for Tut, because he's a really bossy guy, and you need to call Patrick

McMann and tell him to get over here and help. We need to get rid of these people and still make it to school on time. Okay?"

Rafael climbs out of bed. "There's no way this is happening, *especially* this furry scarf thing, but okay. Hey—Tut, get off my phone. Yeah, that's mine. Put it down."

Tut ignores him, and Rafael begrudgingly wraps on the scarf. Then he yells at everyone again, only this time they sort of obey.

"Watch the Viking and Charlie," I tell him. "And call Patrick."

Motioning for Tut to follow me, I head downstairs. As I open the fridge to see what we have, I heard a huge *bang* and *thud* upstairs.

"Off my drum set, Viking! No, off of it!" Rafael yells. "*Luis*! Hurry!"

I sigh. I'm going to be in a lot of trouble if I live through this.

"I'm *starving*," Tut complains for the fiftieth time. He gestures at all of the food in the fridge: chicken, cheese, ketchup, some yogurt, leftover meat loaf. "I don't like any of that. Cook something else."

"Fine," I say. "Just sit down." I open up the freezer to see what's in there and find a box of frozen pizza pockets. Perfect. I spread them out on a tray, and put it in the microwave. Raf and I can have them for breakfast too.

"Don't move," I tell Tut, settling him at the table and handing him two slices of bread to gnaw on. "I'll be right back, and then you can eat."

I hear a noise in the living room and go investigate. The Viking has found my dad's hammer, and he's tapping it against different spots on the wall and listening.

"Put that down! What are you doing? You can't mess up our walls. My mom'll kill me!"

"Looking for your gold. Give it to me now."

I hear a crash from the kitchen and run back in. "Rafael, where are you?" I yell. This is ridiculous. It's like babysitting a bunch of toddlers on sugar.

Tut is calmly munching his bread, but Charlie has appeared, and he's playing with our toaster oven, turning all the dials and making the lights blink on and off. The silverware drawer is upside down on the floor.

"Put the toaster down, Charlie," I say. "Rafael!" I call again. "What's taking so long? Get down here and help me!"

Rafael comes into the kitchen, carrying his smartphone. He starts recording everyone.

"Stop!" I tell him. "We can't have evidence of this. We could get in trouble."

"Why not?" he asks. "We can always pretend it was a play or something."

Charlie, intrigued, moves closer to Rafael and investigates the phone. "What is that device?" he asks.

"It's a telephone, but it's a camera, too. You can take pictures and movies with it."

"Movies? You mean it's a tiny motion-picture camera?" Charlie is amazed. He grabs the phone from Raf and demands that he show him how to use it to make a video.

While they're busy, the pockets finish cooking, and I serve one to Tut and take another one for myself.

"This is good, very good. Make more," Tut demands.

I hand him another from the tray.

"What is it called?" he asks.

"Well, it's like a pizza, but it's folded into a pocket so it's not messy. A pizza pocket. These are pepperoni. There are different flavors."

"Outstanding," he says, chewing.

The back door opens and Patrick walks in. His eyes widen at the sight of everyone in the kitchen. The Viking is having a pizza pocket now too, but he's eating it with his head in the freezer, because he says our house is too hot and he misses the cold breezes of the Arctic Ocean. Tut has pizza sauce all over his face, and Charlie is chasing my brother and filming him with his phone.

"So, this looks pretty bad," Patrick says. "Is your brother flipping out?"

"Ummm, *yes*. I'm pretty sure I'm going to have to give him my allowance for the next year just to keep this quiet."

"Great." Patrick helps himself to a cold enchilada that Tut had pulled out of the fridge and left on the counter. "So what do we do now?"

"That's why you're here. We need a plan." I finish my pizza pocket and wipe my mouth. "Hey, Raf! We need you."

The three of us move into the dining room to talk, leaving our "guests" in the kitchen with two huge plates of food, hoping that will keep them busy and less destructive for a few minutes. I set out a few sodas for them as well, thinking that Tut and the Viking have never had soda before, so it might distract them from tearing my house apart.

"This is bonkers," Raf says. "Mom is going to *kill* me. She said I was in charge of the house and getting you to school this morning, and now look at this place! She probably won't let me go to my basketball game on Saturday."

"We've got bigger problems, Rafael. These guys need to go back to their own time! Immediately! And we've got to return this book to Ms. Tremt so the gloves man doesn't try to steal it again. It's not safe at our house."

"Okay, so return them to their time, Mr. Big Time Traveler," Raf says.

"That's the problem—I don't know how."

"Me neither," says Patrick. "But I guess it's worth a try. We could look up their exact dates and then try to send them through the book, right? Just like Ms. Tremt sent us?"

"Can *we* send other people through the book?" I ask a bit nervously.

Patrick shrugs. "I don't know. We'll find out."

I think it over. Should we send them one at a time, since they're all from different times and places? Or can we just open the book and shove them in anywhere? That's terrible, I know. And I wouldn't do that. I'm just saying. If things get *really* desperate.

"I'll go look up their exact times and places," Rafael offers. "You babysit. And, Patrick, you wear this, er, beautiful scarf so you can try to keep control of them, okay?" He unwraps the orange nano-scarf and hands it to Patrick, who puts it on without complaining. He looks absurd, but then I'm wearing one too, so I guess we can be absurd together.

I'm starting to think Patrick is pretty awesome. Seriously. If we ever make it to school today, I'm going to tell Matt we need to make room for him at our lunch table.

When I go check on the Viking, I find he's tossed all the cushions off the sofa in the living room and has found the handle to the compartment beneath where our sofa bed comes out. He's tugging on it, trying to get it to come up, but one hinge broke when Raf and I were jumping on it a few years ago, and my dad hasn't gotten around to fixing it. So it's really hard to pull up.

The Viking grunts and groans. "This must be your treasure hole! Or you wouldn't have made it so difficult to open!"

"For the last time, Viking, we don't have any treasure! Could you just, you know, sit down? Read a book. Or look at a magazine or something." I pick up a news magazine and shove it into his hands, then turn to Patrick for help.

"Maybe we should call Ms. Tremt," Patrick says. "She can get rid of them. She might be the only one who can."

I mull it over. I wanted to call her right away when I realized that the green-gloves man had been in my house. But if we do, then I have to admit that I stole her book and scarves and brought them home with me. What if she tells me she'll never let me go on another adventure? As scary as yesterday was, and as messy as today is, I don't think I want to be banned forever from time travel. I still want to see the first Olympics in Ancient Greece.

The Viking finally heaves open the sofa bed, and I hear the second hinge pop off. Dad's going to kill me. It's probably better to live to see my teens than to hope to time travel again.

"Fine, call her," I say with a sigh. "I don't think we have a choice."

Patrick goes into the kitchen and picks up the phone. My mom has the main line for school listed on the wall beside it, and Patrick dials. When someone answers, he says, "Hello, can I speak to Valerie Tremt, please? This is her, um, dry cleaner."

He looks at me and shrugs, and I give him the thumbs-up. He's pretty good at thinking on his feet.

A second later he says, "Oh, okay. Thanks."

Looking disappointed, he hangs up and turns to me. "She didn't pick up her line, which means she's either not in the library or not at school yet. And she said they're not allowed to give out her home or cell phone number."

"So we're on our own."

"Unless we want to drag all of them to school and look for her," Patrick suggests.

I picture the Viking riding the school bus, waving his sword and rooting through kids' backpacks for treasure. "Yeah, we're on our own."

CRASH!

Alarmed, I glance at Patrick, and we both run into the foyer to see what's going on. The Viking is now sword-fighting with my dad's overcoat, which is hanging on the back of the coat closet. He's stuck my old stuffed bunny's body into the neck of the coat like a head, and he's poking at it with his sword. The crash was the sound of a lamp, and its bulb is now shattered all over the floor.

"Bad Viking!" I yell.

Then I hear a *Splash! Flush!* and then, "Oh no!" in a panicked English accent. It's coming from the bathroom.

I race there to find Charlie Chaplin staring sadly into the toilet, where Rafael's smartphone is swirling around. It didn't go down with the flush, but it's definitely not going to be in good shape.

"Charlie, *what* are you doing?" Patrick asks.

He smiles sheepishly. "I love the tiny motion-picture camera. I was filming the flush, as an opening sequence for my new film. And I dropped the camera. In the, um, commode."

I close my eyes and shake my head. Can this get any worse? Seriously?

Patrick claps my shoulder. "Stay cool. Help Raf get their dates. I'll fish the phone out and put it in a bowl of rice. Maybe the water will drain out. We won't tell your brother until we have to."

"Okay," I say gratefully. "Thanks."

I go into the kitchen to grab a box of rice for him and find that Tut has decided to pour himself a glass of the soda. Only he spilled it all over the table and then tried to wipe it up with my two favorite Batman comics.

"TUT!" I scream. "What are you doing?"

"Clean this up, boy," he orders. "Your palace is small. And messy."

Just then, Rafael comes downstairs holding a piece of paper, his face white and sick-looking.

"Luis, don't freak," he says. "But I think the Viking just ate your goldfish."

CHAPTER	TITLE
10	Isn't Anybody Homesick?

Time to leave, everyone!" I yell. "Like, right now! Give me the dates, Raf. Patrick, you bring those horribly behaved historical people in here."

Raf hands me the paper with the dates on it. I'm shaking with anger. My goldfish, Joseph, was a prize from the school fair two years ago. I won him at the ring toss, and he's been a very good goldfish. And not many goldfish live for two years or more. He was special. And the Viking *ate* him? What is wrong with that guy?

"We can't wait for Ms. Tremt," I declare. "I'm

going to send them back to any old place. And if they end up in the wrong place, too bad."

Patrick shakes his head. "No, Luis, you can't do that. You could alter history and the world forever! We have to be careful and send them back to the exact time and place they belong. We need Ms. Tremt."

Rafael shakes his head. "We can't wait. You brought them here, Luis, even though you didn't mean to do it. So I'm sure you can figure out how to put them back. Just do it carefully, okay? Don't mess up the entire world."

I think about my goldfish. Poor Joseph. Then I think about the Viking being accidentally set loose in 1950s Paris or something.

I can do it, and do it right. I'm sure I can. "Oh, okay. I was just kidding anyway." I glance at the paper for Tut and see the date *1330 BC*. Yikes! That really is a long time ago. "Get Tut," I instruct Patrick. "I'm going to grab the book."

Still looking dubious, Patrick goes to fetch Tut, and I race upstairs. I move toward my bed, to where I'd stashed the book beneath the mattress for safekeeping, but someone has flipped the mattress over and the book is gone. On the floor beside the mattress is Joseph! He's not moving, but I scoop him up anyway and return him to his bowl. Raf must have seen the empty bowl and just assumed since the Viking was in here that he'd eaten him.

I say a quick prayer and watch as Joseph slowly sinks to the bottom. A second later, he begins to wiggle and finally to swim slowly around the bowl. He's okay!

Phew. I turn around to find the book, but I don't see it anywhere. Could *The Book of Memories* be gone? It has to be here somewhere in this mess. Unless . . . I feel my entire body turn to ice.

Could the green-gloves man have come back?

"Uh, Rafael?" I call downstairs. I don't want to alarm anyone yet, because I'm not positive it's been stolen. "Did you move *The Book of Memories*, by any chance?"

Raf calls up, "Huh? No. Why?"

"No reason," I yell back. *Stay calm*, I tell myself. *Probably the Viking moved it. Or ate it. Or Charlie flushed it down the toilet. I'll just look around for a few minutes, and then I'll panic.*

I begin searching my room, trying not to let my mind wonder about the possibility of the green-gloves man taking it. If he did, then what does he want with it? And what does that mean for the three people mauling my house downstairs? Will be they be stuck in the present forever? With me? Or could I donate them to the Smithsonian, as a kind of living exhibit? Yes, that's exactly what I'll do. I'll donate them to the museum.

I move systematically through my room, checking my bookshelves, my closet, under my bed. No book. Joseph is swimming more energetically now, though, so at least the Viking isn't a fish murderer. That's good news.

What is wrong with me? I need to focus! The book has got to be here somewhere!

"Could you hurry up already?" Rafael calls. "The pizza pockets are gone, and now Tut's hungry again."

"I'm coming, Raf! Just keep him busy, okay?"

I move to Rafael's room and continue my search. I find *his* stash of Halloween candy and eat a chocolate bar for energy. I try not to think about the ticking clock and how we all really need to be getting ready for the bus now or we're going to be biking to school and we'll be late.

I hear a *thud!* and a *whoop!* from the Viking downstairs and shake my head. How on earth did the Viking ships stay afloat with all those destructive people on them?

In my parents' room, I begin digging through a massive pile of my mother's clothes and shoes. Even her suits are wadded up in this pile. She's not going to be happy. I'm nearly at the bottom when my hand passes over the leather cover of a book.

The book!

I shriek with joy and pull it out to examine it. It looks perfectly fine. It's not ripped or wet or burnt to a crisp. It should still work. I think.

I hurry downstairs, holding the book triumphantly over my head. "Got it!" I shout. "I thought the gloved man came back and took it, but he didn't."

"Came back? What do you mean?" Patrick asks. I quickly fill him in, and he looks noticeably disturbed.

"You mean he's the reason these guys are here? I thought it was just because you'd kept the book."

"I don't know," I admit. "But it won't matter in a minute, because I'm about to send them all packing. Hey, Tut! Come here!"

Tut ambles into the living room, looking bored and grumpy. Rafael has turned on the TV, to try to keep the Viking occupied, and now Tut stares at it too, transfixed. Raf put on the Animal Planet channel, and there's a show on about how kangaroos care for their babies.

"Those aren't real," Tut says scornfully.

"They are," I tell him. "They live mostly in Australia."

"Well, I've never seen them in *my* country. Do you have camels here?"

Patrick shakes his head. "Only in zoos. And I saw one once at a Christmas Nativity scene."

"What's Christmas?" asks Tut. "And what are zoos?"

I throw up my hands. "Never mind that now! We're going to send you back home now."

I open up the book and begin to write the place and date for King Tut. But just as my pen starts moving, Tut slaps the book out of my hands and back down onto the floor.

"What?"

"Hey!" Patrick says sharply. "That wasn't nice, King Tut. We're trying to help you."

"I'm not leaving this place," Tut says stubbornly. "I like it here. I like your food. And I like that it's not so hot. My palace is full of people ordering *me* to do things, even though I am the king. My advisers are very bossy. I have to go to prince school. And I'm *tired* and I need a *break*. I'd like to stay here and eat more pizza pockets and look at these pictures of the non-camel animal from Aus-tra-li-a, wherever that is."

"It's another country," I tell him. "Between the Pacific Ocean and the Indian Ocean."

"And it's also a continent," Patrick adds helpfully.

"I will stay here," he says, pointing down at the floor.

I kind of get what he's saying. Maybe it really is tough to be a boy pharaoh ruling Egypt. But at the moment I don't care, because I need to get to first period.

"Listen, King Tut, O wise king," I begin. Patrick smirks and clamps his lips shut, as if trying not to laugh. "I understand that you might like a little, um, vacation. Of course! But the problem is that you're not a king here. When you tell people here who you are, they won't believe you. Just like you didn't believe us about the kangaroos in Australia. In our country, in our time, we don't have kings!"

"No *kings*?" Tut says. "Impossible."

"It's true," I tell him. "People here might even *laugh* at you for pretending to be a king."

"Laugh? At *me*? The greatest pharaoh who has ever ruled Egypt? They wouldn't dare. I'd have them all killed." And he crosses his arms and manages to look very defiant, despite wearing my gray hoodie sweatshirt, which is a size too big on him.

"Who is ruling your country while you're gone? Who will take care of Egypt while you're here?" Patrick asks him.

Tut suddenly looks panicked. He starts pacing. "That cannot happen! You're right—I must go back. Send me back at once, boy."

"Yes, King Tut, I will," I promise. "I'm going to send you all back."

"But first make me one last pizza pocket. Okay? I really have never tasted anything like it. Especially those . . . what did you call them?"

"Pepperonis," Patrick supplies.

"*Delicious*," Tut says. "Pepperonis, pepperonis, pepperonis."

I look at Rafael for his okay and he groans, then heads into the kitchen to make yet another box. My mom will never believe we went through three boxes of pizza pockets in one morning. I'll have to tell her that Patrick came over and he eats a lot.

While Tut is waiting for his last meal in the present, I decide to start working on the Viking, to make sure I can get him to agree to go back.

"Uh, Mr. Viking—" I begin. But I'm cut off by Rafael shouting in the kitchen. *"What happened to my phone?"* Rafael shrieks. *"Charlie?"*

"Yikes, he sounds really mad," Patrick says. "I'll go protect Charlie."

"Thanks," I say gratefully. "I've got some work to do in here. Now, Mr. Viking, I think it's time for you to go back to your ship, wouldn't you agree?"

The Viking peels his eyes from the television long enough to say, "No, I won't. Not until you hand over your gold. That's the Viking rules. We must conquer everyplace we go. That's why we're Vikings."

"Well, you *did* conquer us," I tell him, thinking quickly. "You found my mom's clothes, which are, um, very valuable to her. And my fish, which is my favorite pet ever. And the, uh, secret sofabed pullout. You did great, really."

"I still want to stay," he says defiantly, and turns back to the TV. "There's more treasure here. I know it. You're hiding it from me."

Grrrr. Vikings are so frustrating! What would make him want to return? Tut doesn't want someone else to steal his throne, of course. Maybe it's similar for the Viking?

"Mr. Viking, aren't you worried that you've left your ship for too long? Won't someone try to take it from you, or take over, or steal your, um, whale bones and seal fat?" I try to think of other things Vikings stored on their ships, but my poor brain is tired from all these time-travel screwups.

The Viking stands up. "What did you say? *Who's trying to steal my ship?*"

"No one—yet," I say. "But if you just wait five seconds while I get Charlie ready, then I can send you back to protect it, okay?"

"Be fast, boy, or pay the price." He raises a

hammer at me menacingly.

"You'll have to leave all of this stuff here," I add, pointing at the large afghan full of items the Viking has bunched together beside him. Inside the afghan, which my grandma knitted for me, he's placed a standing lamp, my mother's pearls, a Slinky, a DVD player, and a San Diego Padres baseball cap.

He looks at the afghan mournfully. "I get to keep this hammer, then," he says.

"You keep the hammer," I concede. I think most people would agree, a hammer is a small price to pay to get a Viking out of your house.

Charlie wanders into the room, looking sheepish, and plops down in a chair. I hear Raf yelling at him from the kitchen about his wet phone. I've heard the leave-it-in-a-bowl-of-rice trick only works sometimes, if you're lucky, so no wonder Raf is mad. It might never work again, and it'll take him a long time to earn the money for a new one. Plus, I'll need to buy my dad a new hammer. Dollar signs start flashing before my eyes.

"I didn't mean to ruin the tiny motion-picture camera," Charlie says. "Who knew I'd get so excited and drop it in the commode?" He shakes his head sadly.

"I think it's time for you to go home, Charlie," I tell him. "Back to your movies and the stage and everything you love."

He looks around our house thoughtfully and says, "I'm not so sure. I could do movies here on the tiny camera. If it ever works again. And I really like so many of the things in your house. Your doorbell, the computer, the toaster oven. It's all very marvelous, you see. I can't even get a hot bath most days at my home."

When you hear him describe it, you'd think we lived in a fancy palace like the queen of England, instead of an ordinary split-level house.

"Sorry, Charlie," I say. "Besides, you're going to be incredibly famous! You have so many important films to make, some that change the course of filmmaking forever!" I have no idea what I'm even talking about, but this is the sort of stuff my mom says to me about Charlie Chaplin when she's trying to get me to watch his movies with her.

"All right, then, I suppose," he says, sighing dramatically.

All three of our troublesome visitors line up, and I call Raf back in to watch. I want to make absolutely sure he knows that this book is a time-travel portal and that not one single word of my story was false.

I open the book and write down the first date, for King Tut. The book starts to shimmer a bit and grows a few feet larger, then stops and shrinks right back to normal. I start to panic.

"That's weird," Patrick says. "Try it again."

Rafael looks at the book doubtfully, and I want to shake him and remind him he *did* just see the thing shimmer and get bigger. I write the date, *1330 BC, Armana, Egypt*, again very carefully. And then I focus really hard on it, like I did the last time Patrick and I were trying to get ourselves home.

Just as before, it shakes and shimmers but only gets to be the size of a TV before shrinking back to normal. It's like it's a time-travel window instead of a time-travel door.

"Could you crawl through that tiny window?" I ask Tut, who looks at me like I'm a lunatic.

"I do not *crawl*," he says dismissively. "Ever."

I hand the book to Patrick. "You try it," I tell

him. "Maybe I've got bad vibes or something. After all, I could barely get us home before."

"But that was because of the green-gloves man," he says. "Do you think that's the problem now?"

I throw up my hands in despair. "I don't know. It could be. Unless he broke the book? Try the Viking."

Patrick consults the piece of paper and writes *805 AD, Greenland* into the book. He looks at me, and I cross my fingers. The Viking stands ready, clutching his hammer possessively.

The book does its initial start-up shimmer and starts to grow again. This time it only gets as big as a computer screen.

"It's getting *worse*," Patrick says. "Is it out of power or something?"

"Does it need to be plugged in?" Raf asks, coming forward to examine it.

"No, but maybe it needs to be around Ms. Tremt to work. Maybe she is the source of its power."

Then suddenly I remember the time limit. People who travel through the book must return within three hours. I look at the clock, which reads 8:35 a.m. I have no idea what time everyone came through the book, because I was asleep.

What if it was more than three hours ago and now the book can't send them back?

What if they're all stuck here forever?

Panicked, I look at Patrick. "I think we've missed the time window. That's why the book won't open fully!"

"So what do we do, then?" Raf moans. "We've got school in fifteen minutes, our parents will be home for dinner, and we can't have these three guys living here! Mom and Dad would kill us!"

I mention my idea from earlier to donate them to the Smithsonian museum. No one even cracks a smile.

"We've got to try Ms. Tremt again," Patrick says. "Even if we have to bike to school and find her and bring her back here."

I agree. This is a problem that only a *real* time traveler can handle. I'm just an amateur, at best.

"I'll call the school again," I say, as the oven *dings*.

"That's my pizza pockets," Tut announces. "Put the TV back on so I can watch while I eat, okay?"

I sigh and do as he says. It's 8:35 a.m., and it's already been the longest morning of my life.

While Tut chomps his (hopefully last) pizza pocket, he and the Viking watch TV, and Charlie stares solemnly at Raf's phone submerged in rice, I pick up the house phone to call the school again. Rafael starts to clean up the living room, which I take as a sign that he has faith we'll get these guys out of here. But I'm not so sure anymore.

When Ms. Anderson, the school secretary, answers, I say, "Hello. Can you put me through to Ms. Tremt, please?"

"Certainly, young man," she says, and I hear the sound of Ms. Tremt's line ringing. *Ring, ring, ring.* No answer. Again! Where could she be? Could the green-gloves man have gotten to her?

I hang up. Patrick is beside me, looking worried. "She's still not there?" he asks.

"Nope."

He taps the counter. "I could ride my bike to school and get her. But I wouldn't be back for, like, forty-five minutes. And we'd miss school. And what if she wouldn't come?"

"She'd come," I say. "She gave us the book! And the power to time travel. She'll fix this. We just need to get her here."

"Should we try the SOS again, then?" he says. "It worked when we were stuck before."

When Patrick says "SOS," my brain starts going into overdrive. The SOS we sent was *our* emergency, but what if the *book* had an emergency? The book is a time-travel portal, so it's very valuable. It must be—otherwise, the man with the green gloves, who can already time travel by himself, wouldn't want it. And wouldn't something so valuable, a *treasure*, as the Viking

III

would call it, have some safeguards put on it?

Like Kidd's secret map, which was in a hidey-hole and had a butcher knife booby-trapped to it to protect it from thieves. And I know the United States Constitution and the Declaration of Independence aren't just sitting in ordinary museum cases in Washington, DC: They have all kinds of bullet-proof glass and motion detectors and heat sensors on them, to protect them. Maybe this book is similar. If someone tries to damage it, Ms. Tremt might show up to protect it. It's worth a shot.

I look over at Raf's phone, submerged in its rice bath. All of a sudden I remember what Ms. Tremt told me the other day in the library when she was dusting the smoke detectors. She said *Water is the great enemy of books*. Or did she say, *Water is the enemy of great books*? Either way, she might have been giving me a clue.

"I think I have an idea," I tell Patrick. "We're going to drown it."

"Drown what?" he asks, alarmed.

"*The Book of Memories*! I think if it's in danger, Ms. Tremt will show up automatically to protect it. What do you think?"

"Okay, let's try it," Patrick agrees. "First period is starting now, so we're out of time anyway. If we don't show up at school soon, the office will call our parents."

I grab a large casserole dish from the cabinet and fill it with water. Then I carry the book over to it. Slowly, I show the water-filled dish to the book, as if it were a piglet I was about to bathe. "I'm going to put you in that water, book. So you need to signal your owner, Valerie Tremt, and tell her to get here right now and help us!"

Inch by inch, I bring the book closer to the water, finally dipping one corner into the bath. The second those gold-gilded pages get damp, the kitchen door flies open and Ms. Tremt appears, wearing not one, but *two* of her crazy scarves, her face bright red and flustered.

"Oh my word, Luis!" she exclaims, as she sees me with the book poised over the water. "What on earth are you doing?"

"You came!" I shout. I don't think I've ever been so excited to see anyone in my entire life. I pull the book close to me and hug it, drying the damp corner off with my T-shirt.

"Of course I came. You tried to drown my book!"

Patrick grabs her arm. "Ms. Tremt! We called and called, but we couldn't find you! Help! There are three historical people in the living room and we want to send them home, but we think their time window has closed, and we have to get to first period, and they've destroyed Luis's house!"

Ms. Tremt's eyes grow as large as billiard balls as he speaks. Then she walks to the doorway of the living room and peeks around it. She pulls her head back in. "Oh my. Is that a Viking, King Tutankhamun, and Charlie Chaplin?"

I nod. "Yes. And the Viking is a destructive guest. And Tut is bossy! And Charlie fiddles with everything."

"Yes, yes, that sounds about right. And Luis, we'll discuss your stealing the book from the library at a later time. But for now tell me, how did they get here?"

I quickly tell her about the noises I heard in my room last night and the dream about Kidd wearing the green gloves. "Could it be?" I ask her. "Could the green-gloves man have snuck into my house and tried to take the book?"

Ms. Tremt strokes her two scarves, which are twisted together like a pretzel around her neck. She looks more than a little unnerved. "Yes, Luis and Patrick, I'm afraid so. This is classic Tim Raveltere."

"Tim Raveltere?" Patrick asks. He absently picks up a pizza pocket from the baking sheet on the stove and takes a bite. I don't know how he can eat it. I never want to see or smell them again. "Who in the world is Tim Raveltere? Is he good or bad?"

Ms. Tremt shakes her head. "You know, Patrick, not everyone can be categorized as strictly 'good' or 'bad.' I wish they could. But Tim Raveltere— well, let's just say he's trouble with a capital 'T.' For everyone."

"Why?" I ask.

"He wants the book," she explains. "Desperately. But it was entrusted to *me*, which is why I appear when it's in danger. And also because *I* will only use it for good. But Tim, he wants it to use for his own purposes. He wants to bring back the greatest characters in our world's history and use them to amass power and money, I assume.

But we can't allow that to happen! It would upset the balance of time."

"So he *did* come to try to steal the book . . . but what happened?"

She shrugs. "I don't know. I guess something interrupted him, possibly as he was saying a spell over the book to change its allegiance from me to him. And he accidentally released those three people and didn't have time to put them back."

"But you can? Put them back, I mean?" The clock continues to tick, and every second that goes by we are later for school. Normally I wouldn't mind missing math class, but my parents will find out and they'll never let Raf and me get ourselves ready in the morning ever again. They'll probably get us a *babysitter*.

Ms. Tremt nods smartly. "Yes, indeedy. I can put them back easy enough. The question is what to do about *Tim*. The book is quite safe with me, and at our school. But is it safe for others to travel, now that I know he's capable of this? That I have to figure out."

Rafael appears in the doorway. "Ah, Ms. Tremt. I thought I heard you."

She winks at him. "Hello, Rafael. You didn't believe your brother, did you? And now look! It's quite something, isn't it?"

He groans. "Not exactly my idea of a great adventure."

I interrupt, anxious to get this show on the road. "Uh, Ms. Tremt, could you get them out of here now? Every second they stay, they break something new."

Ms. Tremt laughs and claps her hands. "*Yes,* absolutely. Here we go."

She marches straight into the living room and stares each of them down.

"Gentlemen," she says. "Thank you for your visit. It's been most instructive. However, it's time you went back to your kingdoms and boats and movie sets. Agreed?"

Surprisingly, all three of them are eager to agree with Ms. Tremt, even though they loved arguing with me about every single thing. She must have more power than I think. They all get up from their seats on the couch, where they were watching TV.

"We really should have gotten a picture of the three of them together," Patrick jokes. "We could submit it to the yearbook."

"You could have," Raf says bitterly. "If Charlie hadn't *ruined my phone.*"

Charlie looks down at his feet.

"All right, all right, hand me the book, Luis," Ms. Tremt says, and I do. It's fully dry now, and I'm relieved I didn't have to ruin it to get help.

She opens it up against the wall. But instead of filling out the little card, as she normally does, she raises her hands in front of her like she's about to conduct an orchestra. She closes her eyes and breathes in and out a few times. Then she begins to recite:

> *"NROB EREW UOY EMIT EHT*
> *OT NRUTER.*
>
> *GNOLEB UOY ECALP EHT OT*
> *NRUTER.*
>
> *NROW DNA DLO SKOOL*
> *KOOB SIHT.*
>
> *GNOLA UOY PLEH LLITS*
> *LLIW TI TUB.*

*GNORW SI TNESERP EHT NI
ECNESERP RUOY.*

*RETURN TO THE TIME YOU
WERE BORN.*

*RETURN TO THE PLACE YOU
BELONG.*

*THIS BOOK LOOKS OLD AND
WORN.*

*BUT IT WILL STILL HELP YOU
ALONG.*

*YOUR PRESENCE IN THE
PRESENT IS WRONG."*

The room is absolutely silent for a moment. Then Rafael whispers loudly, "She just said that backward and forward. So she's really not just an ordinary librarian?"

"Apparently not," I whisper back, just as loudly.

"What's happening?" Tut barks.

The book starts to shake and grow (finally!), until we can see the desert and what looks like it might be Armana, Egypt.

"You're first, King Tutankhamun," Ms. Tremt says. "Be good!"

"Tut, before you go, could you leave me the sweatshirt, please?" I ask. "It's one of my favorites."

He sighs and pulls it off over his head, tossing it into a ball on the floor. "I liked your food," he says. "But your house is not very grand." Then he steps through the book and into the desert, and just like that, he's gone.

Ms. Tremt waves, then works her spell again, this time directed at the Viking. He leaves, still clutching his hammer, but none of us dare try to take it from him. Thankfully, he left the afghan full of stuff by the couch.

Last is Charlie, who goes over to Raf first and gives him a hug. "I am so sorry about your tiny motion-picture camera. Come visit me anytime," he says.

Grudgingly, Raf hugs him back. "Aw, it's

okay. It'll probably be fine. Anyway, you are pretty funny. Next time my mom's watching one of your movies, I'll sit down and watch it with her, okay?"

"You are too kind," Charlie says. The book conjures up a large stage, and with a theatrical farewell bow, Charlie disappears as well.

"Now *that's* all taken care of," Ms. Tremt says, dusting off her hands as if she'd just handled a particularly dirty job. "Your house looks a bit worse for the wear, and there's no time to clean it up now. I'll drive you all to school and write you notes for first period, saying that I requested your help in the library this morning."

"Will King Tut, the Viking, and Charlie remember us?" I ask.

"No," Ms. Tremt says. "They will all think they had an amazing dream."

I look at Raf. "We'll have to come straight home today to clean up before Mom and Dad get here," I say. "No basketball. I'm sorry, Raf. And this was all my fault."

"Oh well," he says. "I can skip it one day. And anyway, I guess this was kind of interesting."

"I'll come help too," Patrick offers.

"That's the spirit!" Ms. Tremt says. "You know, one of the reasons I continue to have you kids use the book and time travel is because it puts positive energy into the universe, which ultimately keeps everyone safer."

"Even with this Tim guy out there, sneaking around?" Patrick asks.

"Well, yes. Sometimes things are worth the risk. You see, the book can also lose power if it isn't used regularly, and that would be a terribly tragedy. It's my goal as a librarian, and a time traveler, to spread a love of history to my students. If I can help them connect to the people of the past, it can make everyone's futures brighter."

"That's really nice of you, Ms. Tremt," I say, looking at her in a different light. I resolve not to think of her as kooky anymore. She's . . . magical. And brave.

"Did you think I was just doing it for fun, Luis?" she asks. She grins. "To every thing there is a purpose, and a purpose to every thing."

Raf picks up the book from where it shrunk back down to size by the wall and hands it to

Ms. Tremt. "Take this, please! It shouldn't be in our house for one more minute. And, Luis, my brother, I will never doubt you again."

"Thanks, Raf," I say. "That really means a lot, especially since I had to bring three historical figures into our house and let them nearly destroy it for you to believe me."

"You're a bit of a truth stretcher sometimes," he counters, grinning. "But seriously, you should write all this down, Luis. I mean, you'd have to write it as fiction, because no one but the four of us would ever believe it, but what a story!"

Patrick nods. "And you were so creative when you were coming up with reasons why they should leave! I didn't know you knew so much about history."

Ms. Tremt is beaming. "You know, Luis, I think you may end up finding your treasure after all."

Truthfully, I tell her, "No, Ms. Tremt. I never saw Kidd's map. Not even a peek! The butcher knife fell, and he caught us."

"The *butcher knife*?" she and Raf both say at the same time.

"Oh my," she continues, fanning herself with

one of her scarves. "I didn't know about that part. Regardless, what I meant wasn't that kind of treasure." She taps the side of her head. "It seems to me, you may have discovered the key to unlocking something else that's very valuable. Something you'll understand in time."

Baffled, I just stare at her, until Raf reminds us we need to leave in the next two minutes or we'll miss second period, too. With a last look around the house, we file out after Ms. Tremt.

I'm already wondering if I can take a nap at lunch. Time travel is pretty exhausting. Even when you don't actually travel.

CHAPTER	TITLE
12	Luis's Surprising Discovery

Thanks to Ms. Tremt, we show our notes to our second-period teachers and don't get in trouble. And she personally goes to Ms. Anderson to make sure our parents hadn't been called and to tell her we'd been helping her with a special project in the library.

I try to concentrate in class all day, but it's hard to listen to Ms. Castine droning on and on about Ancient Greece when I know now that if I *really* want to learn about what it was like to live in Ancient Greece, I could just go back there and visit.

And I wish I could tell my class that pirates are, well, pretty pirate-y, but they're also neat guys. And being on a ship is dangerous, smelly, hard work, and even though it seems like such an adventurous way to live, it was probably pretty miserable most of the time. Just the body lice alone would be awful! And wearing belt buckles carved from stale biscuits.

At lunch, instead of going to my usual table, I sit with Patrick. He doesn't say anything, and I don't say anything, but I know we'll be friends now, for a long, long time. When my regular lunch buddies, Matt and Grace, see me at a different table, they just pick up their trays and come join us too. Patrick doesn't say anything, but I can tell he's pleased. I wonder why I didn't make more of an effort to get know him before. I guess because he was new and I already had my group of friends. Now he's one of them.

Finally the school bell rings and it's the end of the day. Patrick finds me at my locker and rides the bus home with me. We meet Raf a block away from home.

"Just how bad was the mess?" Raf asks. "Do you remember?"

"It wasn't good," I say. "Especially Mom's clothes. How are we going to explain all the wrinkles?"

"Hang all of her clothes up in the bathroom. Then turn the shower on hot and close the door," Patrick says. "Let the steam get the wrinkles out. That's what my mom does. She hates to iron."

"Wow! That's a great idea." Raf looks impressed. "You do that while Luis works on the kitchen, and I'll work on the living room. And we can do our rooms last, since they're always messy anyway."

"Not *that* messy," I say. "The Viking . . ."

As soon as I say "the Viking" all three of us burst out laughing, since it seems so odd now, after a completely ordinary day at school, to be talking about the real-life Viking that was running us ragged this morning.

"I hope we don't forget everything that happened," I say. "It's too funny."

"Write it down, Luis," Raf says again. "I'm serious—only you could tell it the right way."

"I'll think about it," I say.

When we get to my house, we all clamber

inside. Raf looks at this watch and says, "Okay. It's three forty-five p.m. Mom is usually here by five twenty p.m. That means we have ninety-five minutes. Everyone knows their assignments. GO!"

We end up getting the housework done with minutes to spare. My parents' bedroom looks mostly fine, though there's a strange lingering smell we can't figure out. My bedroom and Raf's look normal, and my goldfish is still alive. The living room has one noticeable dent in the wall from the hammer, but Raf has decided to say we did it throwing the football around. The afghan my grandmother knitted has a hole in it, but it's not terrible. The kitchen is clean, and the trash is taken out. Raf's phone isn't working yet, but it's still drying out in its rice bath.

Patrick high-fives us on his way out and heads home. "See you tomorrow?" he asks as I wave good-bye. I get the feeling what he's really asking is if we're friends now for good.

"For sure," I say.

Raf goes upstairs to start his homework, and so do I. Nothing puts our parents in a better mood than coming home from work to find us both studying.

But I find that when I sit down at my desk, where the book lay only hours before, I can't concentrate on my math worksheet. All I can think about is everything that's happened in the last two days. And Raf's right—if I don't write it all down, we might lose the details of this crazy adventure.

So even though I've never really thought of myself as a writer, I open up my laptop and start a new document.

Two Kids Meet Captain Kidd—

A Harrowing Adventure at Sea

It all started in 1698, aboard the Quedagh Merchant, *one of the ships captured and seized by the infamous pirate Captain William Kidd. . . .*

As I type, the words pour out of me, faster than I can even get them down. It's almost as if the story has been waiting for me to sit down and write it! By the time I hear my mom calling that dinner is ready, I've already got four whole pages, and I have so much more to say.

Maybe Ms. Tremt was right. Maybe I did a find a treasure on my trip—only it isn't the gold and shiny kind. It's that I love to tell stories. Me, Luis Ramirez, a writer!

"Raf, Luis, dinner!" Mom calls again.

Mom gives me a hug when I enter the kitchen, and I squeeze her back harder than usual, because I'm so happy to see her and not a Viking in our house. "What's for dinner?" I ask.

With a flourish, she turns around and shows me the two boxes of takeout pepperoni pizza on the counter.

I plaster a huge smile on my face, because if my mom saw that I wasn't excited to eat pizza, she'd probably call our pediatrician. But inside, all I can think about are those dozens of pizza pockets King Tut ate in our kitchen that morning.

Honestly, I'd give anything for a plain old peanut butter sandwich.

CAPTAIN WILLIAM KIDD

Captain William Kidd was a Scottish sailor and privateer who was tried and executed for piracy. He is one of the most famous pirates in history, primarily because of his execution, but also because it is believed that most of his treasure was never found and is still hidden somewhere along the New Jersey coast (possibly in Cape May, Toms River, or Sandy Hook) and off the coast of Madagascar. About a million dollars' worth of his treasure has previously been found located off Gardiner's Island, which is near Long

Island. Kidd, who was born in Scotland in 1645, began his career as a privateer hired by European royals to attack foreign ships. However, after a two-year dry spell with very little loot to show for their troubles, his crew threatened to mutiny and pressured him to attack a five-hundred-ton Armenian ship, the *Quedagh Merchant*. Kidd agreed, conquering the ship and sailing it home to the United States, where he was promptly arrested for piracy. He was eventually executed, and to serve as a warning to other pirates, his body was hung in a cage and left to rot along the River Thames in London.

VIKINGS

When you hear the word "Vikings," you probably picture large, fierce men with beards and horned helmets. Well, that's somewhat true. "Vikings" is the name by which Scandinavian seaborne raiders in the early medieval period are commonly known. They were warriors, and very fierce. But they didn't generally wear the horned helmets they are often associated with. Instead, they wore the trousers and shirts regular men wore, and for battle added leather body protectors and shirt mail if they had it. Very few metal helmets with nose plates have been found by historians, making it likely they were worn only by the rich and powerful. Vikings were believed to be quite hygienic, bathing approximately once a week, which was more than most people at the time. It was apparently quite popular to be blond if you were a Viking, as many would bleach their hair using a strong soap with a high lye content.

KING TUTANKHAMUN (KING TUT)

King Tut was born in approximately 1341 BCE, and was the twelfth king of the eighteenth Egyptian dynasty. Known as the "boy king," since he ruled as pharaoh from the ages of about nine to eighteen, his death mask resides in the Egyptian Museum in Cairo and remains one of the most famous and recognizable of all Egyptian artifacts, even though he reigned for only about eight or nine years and accomplished relatively little. However, the discovery of his nearly intact tomb in 1922 received massive press coverage and reignited a worldwide interest in Ancient Egypt. King Tut was believed to have suffered from many ailments, including a club foot and Kohler disease.

CHARLIE CHAPLIN

Charlie was a comedic British actor who became famous in the early 1900s for his silent movies. One of his most famous characters, The Tramp, was a sweet little man with a bowler hat, mustache, and cane. The Tramp relied on pantomime and quirky movements to entertain his fans. As one of the first superstars of the movie industry, Charlie went on to become a director, making films such as *City Lights* and *Modern Times*, and cofounded the United Artists Corporation. He was known as a total perfectionist. He loved to experiment and often required countless takes to get a scene right. It was not uncommon for him to order the rebuilding of an entire set or to fire a leading actor after they'd begun filming a movie because he realized he'd made a mistake in his casting.

CHAPTER 1
Being Graceless

I can feel it coming. That awful feeling you get when you know someone is talking about you and that they're not saying nice things. Do you know that feeling? If you do, I'm really sorry, because honestly, it's the worst. The sad thing is, I've been getting that feeling more and more lately. And I'm not really a conspiracy-theorist kind of girl. So I'm sort of thinking people really are talking about me more. And by people, I mean my fellow students at Sands Middle School.

"Grace, watch out for that . . . ," Matt warns me.

"Step," he is about to say. But I miss the bottom step before Matt can get the word out. I fall flat onto my face and my books go flying. Again.

"That's the third time this week!" I moan.

"Maybe your feet are still stuck in 1951," Luis whispers.

"Or your balance," Matt chimes in, smiling.

I hope you don't get the wrong impression about Luis and Matt. They're totally great guys, and I've been friends with them forever. They'd do anything for me, and I would for them. But it's easier for them to laugh off an uncomfortable situation, like watching me fall on my face, than to deal with real feelings. Which I know is their way of trying to make it all seem not so bad. And it wouldn't be, except for the crowd of other kids that just saw my free fall.

I try to get myself back up to standing again without making too much of a scene, but since that involves my foot sliding across one of the books I've just dropped, in the middle of lifting myself to a standing position . . . Well, you can imagine it's not a very pretty picture. Good thing I didn't wear a skirt today.

And maybe Luis has a point. Maybe my feet are stuck in 1951. Because you would think that after having the kind of once-in-a-life-time, mind-blowing experience like the one we just had, I'd have come out differently on the other side of it. A little wiser . . . a little more polished . . . and definitely with the ability to put one foot in front of the other and not trip over it. Except in my case, not.

I can't tell you too much about it, time-traveler code of honor and all, but if you're wondering where all this talk about 1951 comes from, let me give you a hint. It involves a book, a librarian, Matt's grandfather, and a trip that I would have never believed possible. Confused? Join the club. I'm still not sure that it even was possible. But more on that later. Right now, back to the awful feeling.

I don't even have to guess that the buzzing murmurs from the crowd mean they're all talking about me, because it's so obvious that they are. They're not even trying to hide it anymore. I can feel my cheeks burning as Matt and Luis hand me the books they have just collected from across the hall floor.

"Move it, klutz," Jason Coppola says with a laugh as he pushes past me, almost causing me to toss my books again.

"What's up, Graceless?" Jessica Flannery laughs from in front of her locker.

"What's your problem, Jessica?" Matt snarls.

You gotta love that kid. I know Matt thinks that I don't know kids have been calling me Graceless since second grade. He's sweet like that. But if I didn't know about that nickname, they could call me Clueless, too. It's not that big of a leap of creativity, really. Grace—Graceless, I'm not impressed.

I am embarrassed to be living up to their stupid nickname, though. And my heart feels like it's being squeezed in someone's hand when I notice that in the midst of Jessica Flannery's giggling fan-girl group is Morgan Stevens.

I've known Morgan since the fourth grade, when we were both into the same fantasy book series: DragonDamsels. We used to spend hours talking about the damsels in our rooms, we'd doodle in each other's notebooks, and we even took an oath to never tell anyone but each other our DragonDamsel names. (Sorry, I can't do it. Even if she is laughing at me now, I will never break that oath.) Last year when Morgan was having trouble in history class, we spent hours together in the library reviewing Roman Empire facts. She ended up getting an eighty-nine in the class with my help. Et tu, Morgan?

So the feeling—that feeling—well, it's a little hard to hide right now. I can feel the tears collecting in the ducts underneath my eyes, so I tell Matt and Luis I need to stop at the bathroom before I go to class. All I have to say is "girl stuff" and they scurry away as if I just told them I had the measles.

Once I pull myself together, the rest of morning isn't very eventful. All of my teachers are happy to see me—they always are. I'm happy to have schoolwork to focus on, and even if my classmates aren't as happy about the work as I am, at least it keeps them busy.

I will admit, there are a couple of times when I think I hear my name, or my nickname, whispered in the back of the classroom, but I could be wrong, so I am choosing to ignore it.

Until lunchtime, that is. The thing with being super clumsy, which I have no problem admitting that I am, is that the more you think about it and the more you try to overcome your natural tendencies, the more anxious you become about them. And then that anxiety fuels those tendencies like anger fuels the Hulk and well . . . clumsy to the infinitesimal power is the result.

I know the anxiety's going to start the second I step foot into the lunchroom. I try to do some of the strategies I practiced with my dad. I stop, take a deep breath, and keep my eyes focused on the goal.

The goal is: Grab a lunch tray, choose the least offensive food offerings, and carry it to a table, hopefully one where no one who would be whispering about me is sitting. I tackle the first two steps successfully. Even though beef patties aren't my favorite item, they are a lot more edible than the cardboard-flavored pizza that is baking under the cafeteria's hot lamps. I grab a side salad and fill a little cup up with dressing. Sometimes I slip and miss the little cup, but today there is not even a drip down the side. I sigh with relief.

I'm feeling pretty good, so I keep my eyes focused on my target—an empty table—as I walk past Jessica Flannery. I hear something squish underneath my feet, but I am determined to just get to the table and ignore everything that might distract me. Until I hear Jessica shriek.

"Way to go, Graceless," Jessica moans. "You just got ketchup all over my new boots. Thanks a lot!"

I look down and see that she's right. The squishing sound came from a ketchup packet I'd inadvertently stepped on. I mean, it's not really my fault, because I wasn't the one who put the ketchup on the floor, but I don't think Jessica's going to buy that argument.

"I'm sorry, Jessica," I say. "I didn't see the packet there. Is there something I can do to help?"

"Yeah," Jessica says. "Stay away from me. As far away as you can get."

The girls at Jessica's table all roll their eyes and giggle.

"My mom is going to freak when she sees this," Jessica tells them. "These boots cost mucho dinero."

Jessica's words, and the giggling, echo in my

head as loud as an ambulance siren. I look over at Morgan and her eyes quickly dart away from mine. Forget Graceless. I'm Hopeless!

I take my tray over to the empty table and slump down onto the bench. I don't feel like eating anymore. Matt and Luis come and sit next to me. If they saw what happened with Jessica, they're doing a good job pretending they didn't. Matt starts to talk about his big game later that afternoon. It's time for me to tune out.

I settle into my seat and realize that I feel so alone. It's strange. I have two great friends sitting on either side of me. I'm in a lunchroom filled with laughing kids whom I've had good times with in the past. But right now, in this moment, I am like my pet snail, Swifty, during the winter—trapped alone inside my shell.

"Earth to Grace! Are you in there?" Luis calls into my ear.

"I'm here." I smile at him. "I just have a lot on my mind."

"Sure you do." Luis laughs. "Or you just find Matt's baseball talk as boring as I do."

"Hey!" Matt protests. "I thought you guys like baseball now!"

"We do," I tell Matt.

"So come check out my game after school today," Matt says. "I'm pitching, you know."

"Not today, Matt," I say. "I'm going to go home and read. I'm really into this new book."

"Oh yeah," Luis says. "Which one?"

"Um . . . I can't remember the title right now. I left the book home," I say, flustered, because I can't even think right now.

"Right," Matt says disbelievingly. "No worries, Grace. We're here if you need us."

"Always," I say. "I know."

That afternoon when the dismissal bell rings, I keep my head down as I scurry toward my locker and quickly pack up my books. I just want to blink my eyes, disappear from Sands Middle School, and reappear safe inside my own bedroom, but I don't have any magical books to transport me at the moment. It's up to me, and only me, to get from my locker, through the crowded halls, and out the school doors without any major mishaps. Fingers crossed.

I'm actually doing a pretty good job of zig-zagging through the daily throng of middle schoolers desperate for some social interaction without being noticed. Now I just have to get past the library and down the stairway, and them home free! Except . . .

THWACK! CRASH! BANG!

I'd like to ignore the commotion coming from inside the library, but given my recent history in there, I just can't. And when Ms. Tremt, our school librarian, appears at the door, her usually perfect hair looking like a bird's nest and her crazily colorful scarf almost falling off her neck, I know my dreams of getting to my room are doomed.

"Is everything okay?" I ask Ms. Tremt.

"It will be, Grace," she replies. "But at the present time, sadly, it is not."

"What's not?" I ask. "Maybe I could help?"

Ms. Tremt takes a step closer to me and then leans her face toward mine. She stares into my eyes, her nose nearly touching my nose. If it were anyone else, I'd be busting out laughing right now, but it's Ms. Tremt, and she's looking so super serious that I'm getting a little nervous.

"You know, Grace," Ms. Tremt finally says, so close that I can feel the breath she takes with each word. "I believe you may be able to."

She begins explaining the problem to me. It involves Ms. Tremt's glowing, magical pen. I know that I said before that I am bound by the time-traveler code of honor, but if I don't explain this, you're going to be totally lost, so here it goes. . . .

Matt, Luis, and I found out the truth about Ms. Valerie Tremt not very long ago. The first clue was her name. Check it out—if you unscramble the letters, they also spell out "time traveler." And that's the truth. Our librarian, who seems a little zany with her wacky colorful scarves and her instinctual ability to put exactly the right book into each of our hands, is actually a time traveler. Or rather, a time-travel facilitator, at the very least. Because while I haven't actually seen Valerie Tremt travel through time, she was the reason that Matt, Luis, and I got to travel back to 1951. Are you following me? Good, because I know it's a lot.

The way we got to time travel was by using Ms. Tremt's special magical pen to write in The Book of Memories. It's like this weird portal to the past (and maybe future, who knows?), but it's also an actual book, and you need to "sign it out" using the magical pen and writing the details of your destination. You know, time, place, that kind of stuff.

Anyway, Ms. Tremt cannot find the pen and she has searched high and low, but sometimes she can be a little scattered, so I suggest that we do a systematical search again. I may be clumsy in my movements, but my brain is a nimble beast.

Ms. Tremt, however, seems to be really scattered at the moment. She keeps mumbling something that sounds like, "tim-rah-vel-teer." I'm not sure if that is some secret time-traveling chant, or a foreign language phrase, but the way Ms. Tremt is saying it gives me the feeling that it's not a good thing.

"Ms. Tremt," I interrupt. "We need to focus. Now think hard. Where is the last place you remember using the pen?"

Ms. Tremt starts mumbling to herself again, and I'm sure she says "Patrick" and "Luis" in there, but she clearly doesn't want to tell me the details, so I decide we'd better try another strategy—divide and conquer!

"Let's divide the room into levels," I suggest. "We can start with the bottom level first, in case it fell on the floor or rolled off a table, and then move up from there."

"An excellent plan," Ms. Tremt agrees.

We split up, head to opposite sides of the room, and get on our hands and knees. Crawling around the library floor isn't exactly how I'd planned to spend my afternoon, but at least there's no danger of me tripping.

It turns out there is danger, though, and it's hiding behind the historical fiction bookshelf. That's where I find this massive grumpy guy, looking like he's walked out of the pages of Viking Explorers. He's got a thick, furry red beard, a giant sword and shield, and a winged metal hat.

"Oh, great, Erik," Ms. Tremt moans.

"As in, 'Erik the Red?'" I ask.

"The one and only," Ms. Tremt replies.

The Norwegian explorer looks like he's a little lost, and not very happy about it. He grumbles and growls and knocks over stacks of books and topples tables and chairs.

"I think he's looking for his Viking warriors," Ms. Tremt whispers.

"Are they here, too?" I ask.

"They don't seem to be." Ms. Tremt sighs. "Which is a relief. But this . . . this is a very big problem, Grace."

"I'm starting to see that," I agree. "Can you send him back?"

"Not without my pen," Ms. Tremt says.

Erik is making a big mess in the library, and it's more doubtful than ever that we'll actually find Ms. Tremt's pen. So my logical brain starts to buzz again.

"We need a plan B," I tell Ms. Tremt. "He

looks like a powerful guy. Maybe you could put him to work here."

"He's a little too rough with the books," Ms. Tremt says.

"I wasn't thinking he'd make a great librarian." I laugh. "But he looks like he'd be a good gym teacher. Look at the way he's using his sword and shield—I bet the girls lacrosse team could learn a thing or two from him."

"I like the way you think, Grace." Ms. Tremt smiles. "If I can't find the pen by tomorrow morning, Sands Middle School may have a new substitute coach on the lacrosse field."

"And in the meanwhile?" I ask.

"I'd better start researching some Viking recipes, because it looks like I'll be cooking for Erik the Red tonight." Ms. Tremt laughs.

"Well, you'd better get started on that at home," I say, "before he does any more damage in here."

Ms. Tremt heads over to Erik the Red, takes his hand, and stares into his eyes. She definitely has an instantly calming effect on the Viking.

"One last thing," I call to her as she heads out

of the library. "Whenever I forget where I put things, it's always because my mind is on something else . . . usually something I'm worried about. So if you can, try to get that thing out of your head for a while, and then you might be able to remember the last place you had your pen."

"I will try, Grace," Ms. Tremt says, waving good-bye. "I will certainly try."